She couldn't move

Euan seemed to be as still as she was. It was a blink of time but more than long enough for something to click into place.

It wasn't conscious. It had to be the result of a lot of things. Things like how excited Abby was to be here, in this spectacular place. The way Euan's story had captured her heart so firmly. Her determination to try to do something to help him. The fact that, despite his outward grumpiness and the impression he wasn't that happy to have her here, there was a level of attraction that was the final catalyst for what Abby realized might be the perfect way to make this Christmas more enjoyable for this man.

She hadn't lowered the mistletoe, which was the perfect excuse for what she did next.

Abby stood on her tiptoes and kissed him.

She'd only intended it to be a friendly sort of kiss. A brief, under-the-mistletoe, Christmassy sort of kiss. One that wasn't going to be significant in any way.

But the instant her lips touched his, everything changed…

Dear Reader,

I couldn't write the books I write unless I truly believed in romance—in the magic of finding that soul mate and falling in love—but there are other themes in my stories, and I think the strongest one is that of family and home. That's also all about love.

I believe love is the binding force that creates the most powerful connection there is. It can be totally unexpected or grow from an unlikely combination of things and, sadly, it isn't something that everybody is lucky enough to find. It's invisible and so powerful it can change whole worlds, and if that isn't real magic, I don't know what is.

Euan McKendry finds Christmas beyond difficult. But there's a unique alchemy this Christmas that is going to change his world forever. There's a castle. And snow. Children. And Abby, who looks like a Christmas angel. And there's magic happening. The magic of more than one kind of love…

I think this might be one of my favorite books ever. I really hope you enjoy reading it as much as I did writing it.

Happy Christmas!

Alison Roberts xxx

CHRISTMAS MIRACLE
AT THE CASTLE

———

ALISON ROBERTS

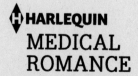

HARLEQUIN
MEDICAL
ROMANCE

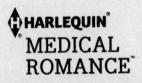

Recycling programs
for this product may
not exist in your area.

ISBN-13: 978-1-335-40895-2

Christmas Miracle at the Castle

Harlequin Enterprises ULC
22 Adelaide St. West, 40th Floor
Toronto, Ontario M5H 4E3, Canada
www.Harlequin.com

Printed in U.S.A.

Alison Roberts is a New Zealander, currently lucky enough to be living in the south of France. She is also lucky enough to write for the Harlequin Medical Romance line. A primary-school teacher in a former life, she is now a qualified paramedic. She loves to travel and dance, drink champagne, and spend time with her daughter and her friends.

Books by Alison Roberts

Harlequin Medical Romance

Twins Reunited on the Children's Ward

A Pup to Rescue Their Hearts
A Surgeon with a Secret

Royal Christmas at Seattle General

Falling for the Secret Prince

Medics, Sisters, Brides

Awakening the Shy Nurse
Saved by Their Miracle Baby

The Paramedic's Unexpected Hero
Unlocking the Rebel's Heart
Stolen Nights with the Single Dad

Visit the Author Profile page
at Harlequin.com for more titles.

For Becky

With so much love and happy memories of
magical Christmas moments xxx

**Praise for
Alison Roberts**

"Ms. Roberts has delivered a delightful read in this
book where the chemistry between this couple was
strong from the moment they meet...the romance
was heart-warming."

—*Harlequin Junkie* on
Melting the Trauma Doc's Heart

CHAPTER ONE

THERE WAS NO doubt about it—this was going to be the best Christmas *ever*.

The sheer joy of seeing the first, fat flakes of snow drifting down onto the high street in Inverness, Scotland, stopped Dr Abby Hawkins in her tracks. With a level of excitement that was probably more appropriate for one of her small patients in a paediatric ward, she tilted her face to stare up at the slate-grey sky. She had the presence of mind to behave well enough not to poke out her tongue, but she did hold out her gloved hands, palm upwards, hoping to catch some flakes that way. She knew she was creating a bit of an obstacle on one side of a footpath crowded with Christmas shoppers, but it was simply irresistible to savour this moment of pure magic.

'Never seen snow before, lassie?'

Abby's head swerved fast enough for her to identify that the speaker was the driver of a taxi amongst traffic that had ground to a halt beside her.

'Not for Christmas,' she told the taxi driver. It felt as if she were smiling from ear to ear. 'Not in New Zealand.'

'You're a long way from home, then.' The traffic was lurching back into motion so he began sliding his window shut. 'Aye, well… you'd best make the most of it. Might be pretty enough now but it'll turn to slush. It always does…'

The window closed with an audible clunk and the wave over his shoulder as he departed looked more like a gesture of dismissal, but Abby wasn't about to let that kind of attitude from a Christmas Grinch spoil the moment. Nothing could spoil this. The snow was falling more thickly and it was beginning to coat things, like the shiny red top of a mail box nearby and Abby couldn't remember the last time she'd felt quite *this* excited.

She'd been spot on to choose to come to the north of Scotland, thinking that it would offer her the best chance to have a white Christmas for the first time in her life. No, that wasn't quite true, was it? The choice had really been made well before she'd thought of that particular bonus. In fact, she'd been so captured by the unusual advertisement she'd seen in the professional careers opportunities section of *The Lancet* that she would have applied even if it had been a Christmas camp set in the middle of the Sahara Desert with zero chance of experiencing a decent snowfall.

Because Christmas was all about children and these were special kids that were being treated to a fantasy Christmas. Kids that had congenital heart problems, family circumstances that ranged from difficult to appalling and, as if that weren't already a heart wrenching situation, they were also sick enough to need expert medical staff available twenty-four-seven. It was a marriage made in heaven. Abby not only adored being with children, she had just spent a year in London, completing a year of specialist paediatric cardiology training and she was taking a short break to think about exactly what she wanted in her next position. She also adored everything to do with Christmas and, as if that combination weren't perfect enough, this unexpected five-day gig was happening in a castle that looked as if it had come straight out of a fairy tale with its stone walls and turrets, a lake and a forest in its extensive estate and a dramatic backdrop of rugged looking mountains.

Abby had forgotten all about the grumpy, Grinchy taxi driver as she ducked across the road, heading for a pharmacy. She couldn't be happier. Except that she'd accidentally left her toilet bag behind in the B&B she'd stayed in last night to break the long journey and she couldn't turn up at the castle and ask to be provided with shampoo and toothpaste and makeup and even a hairbrush, could she? There were other things she only realised she needed to add to her basket as she spotted them on the shelves and some things that had definitely not been left behind in her toilet bag—like the wearable decoration of a small elf, his legs forming part of the headband's curve. His arms were outstretched, he had a huge grin on his face and there was a real bell on top of his hat that would jingle merrily when the wearer moved their head. The children she would be caring for would love that, wouldn't they?

Never mind the kids… Abby loved it herself. She had long suspected that there was a part of her that had never quite grown up but that was often a good thing in her line of work, because she could explain things to older children in a way they could understand and she had a knack of finding ways to distract any child or baby from a frightening or unpleasant medical intervention, and even make them laugh sometimes. It was always more noticeable at this time of year, of course, because she could so easily tap into the magic of Christmas with all the joy of a child.

And it was going to be on a totally different level this time. So different, it felt… huge. As if being accepted for this position was an honour. That she was privileged to be part of something that would be creating a memory like no other for these children and the people who loved them. After reading up on the information she'd been provided with, Abby knew that for some of the children coming to this Christmas camp at the castle, it was a miracle that they were actually having another Christmas. Most would be coming with carers or parents and siblings—the people who were living with the fear that serious illness could bring so they deserved to share a very special celebration. It was enough to mean Abby needed to swallow a rather large lump in her throat. She couldn't wait to meet Margaret McKendry, who must be a rather special woman having apparently been making this happen for twenty-five years now. She couldn't wait to meet the children and the rest of the team who would be caring for them and she was hanging out for a first glimpse of the castle.

She just couldn't wait, full stop. Abby was itching to get back on the road that led to the village of Kirkwood and on to Ravenswood Castle as soon as possible so her heart sank a little as she saw the length of the queue to get to the check-out counter. She had no choice than to take her place at the back, however, and wait patiently behind a tall man in a black woollen beanie hat and puffer anorak, who was focused intently on the screen of the phone he was holding.

There was no doubt about it. This was shaping up to be the worst Christmas ever and that was saying something when Euan McKendry had learned to dread the festive season so many years ago he'd barely been in his teens.

The meteorological website he was scanning was forecasting heavy snow showers for the next twenty-four to thirty-six hours. It would clear by Christmas Eve but, by then, there would probably be snow drifts deep enough to bury cars and/or people. It would be bitterly cold and he would, as always, be sleeping in that turret that had drafts whistling through the gaps around those mullioned windows.

One of these days, Euan promised himself, he would go and spend Christmas on the beach. In Australia. Or New Zealand. Somewhere he could soak up the sun and have a barbecued Christmas dinner of steak or prawns, perhaps, instead of turkey and bread sauce. He could swim in the surf, feel the sand between his bare toes and not have a care in the world. One day, he wouldn't have to steel his heart to cope with all the sad memories or having his heartstrings pulled as tightly as piano wire by the stories and personalities of not only sick but disadvantaged children.

But it wouldn't be this year. Not when this could be the last Christmas camp that his grandmother, Maggie, would be well enough to host in the astonishing castle that was her home and she had told him how much she needed him to be there.

'Just one more time, Euan. It's the twenty-fifth anniversary of that first time. Please come...this is for Fiona, after all...it's always been for Fiona and, if this is going to be the last time, I want it to be absolutely the best ever.'

No... Euan tried to stave off the inevitable pull back in time. He wasn't going to start thinking about the younger sister he'd lost so long ago. He wasn't even going to dwell on the fact that his beloved grandmother was awaiting results on a biopsy that probably wouldn't come until after Christmas now but the surgeon had warned her the news might not be good. If it was an ovarian cancer, it was well advanced and the prognosis was poor.

'If this is going to be the last time...'

Euan could actually hear the echo of his gran's voice in his head from that phone call last night and, if he wasn't careful, he might end up standing in this queue—waiting to pick up the prescription pain medication he'd decided to add to his medical kit at the last minute—with tears running down his face. And he wasn't about to let that happen. He hadn't let it happen in twenty-five years. He might not have inherited Maggie's remarkable ability to face the hardest parts of life with a dogged determination to find something to be thankful for, that silver lining she insisted was there somewhere, even in the darkest of clouds, but he could do what he was very, very good at doing. He could keep that door in his heart firmly locked and avoid the kind of emotions he never wanted to grapple with again.

It might have been difficult to distract himself completely from the worry of what those biopsy results would show, or the fact that he was adding a powerful analgesic to his kit because his gran might be in a lot more pain than she was admitting to, if he hadn't been actually jolted hard enough to prevent him thinking about anything other than what was happening in this moment.

Someone had pushed him from behind, hard enough to make him almost lose his balance. His phone flew from his hand to land with an ominous crash on the tiled floor of this old pharmacy. There was a much louder crash at the same time.

'Oh... I'm *so* sorry...'

Euan ignored the woman directly behind him in the queue because he was scanning the whole scene, automatically assessing where his attention was needed first. Further back in the queue, a man was standing with his fists raised.

'This is a *queue*. You don't push in, mate,' he was shouting. 'Got it?'

Another man was on the floor, sitting amongst a pile of hair products that had fallen off the shelf he'd obviously been pushed into. No wonder other people had hastily tried to get out of the way of the falling containers and boxes so it was no fault of the woman with the unusual accent that she'd bumped into him so abruptly. It possibly wasn't the fault of the man who was now picking himself up from the floor, either. Maybe he'd only wanted to get to the other side of the queue to buy some shampoo but fortunately he wasn't about to engage with the angry customer protecting his place in the line. He got up and headed for the door as stressed looking pharmacy staff were rushing in to clear the mess.

Euan shook his head in bemusement, swore under his breath and bent to retrieve his phone, which had been stopped from sliding further away by a basket someone had put down on the floor. He wasn't surprised to see the deep, jagged crack on the screen of his phone after how loud the impact had been but his heart sank a little further. There was no chance he could get that fixed before heading out of Inverness so it would be a pain to use the device for at least a week. At the same moment he was noting what was going to be a serious nuisance, something in his peripheral vision caught his attention and it instantly added insult to injury. On the top of that almost full basket was one of those ridiculous bits of Christmas nonsense that people made a point of putting on their heads, like reindeer horns, or miniature Santa hats. This had to be the worst example he'd ever seen—a stupidly grinning elf who had his arms outstretched as if he was ready to hug anyone and everyone.

It was so horrible that, as Euan straightened again, he couldn't help looking behind him at the person who was about to purchase it. The same person who'd just apologised for shoving him in the back. He knew that he might not be disguising how he felt about someone who would choose to buy such an idiotic stuffed toy to wear on their head but he didn't care. Maybe he would be doing her a favour and she'd decide to leave it behind. His look, which was admittedly probably more like a glare, clearly surprised the woman but it was backfiring badly for Euan because *he* was even more surprised.

Gobsmacked, in fact.

He was staring at what had to be the most beautiful woman he'd ever seen in his life.

Huge, blue eyes framed by a tangle of dark lashes. A generous mouth that had clearly been designed with laughter and smiling in mind and her lips were clearly on the brink of curling right now, because she was not only gorgeous but she appeared to be quite possibly the *happiest* woman Euan had ever seen and that glow was only enhanced by her long, long blonde hair that fell in soft waves from beneath her red woollen hat. The hat didn't look quite right, did it? A shining halo might have been more appropriate because, whoever this was, she looked like a Christmas angel that had suddenly come to life.

Good grief…

She was definitely smiling at him now.

And, dammit, but it was making her look even more beautiful. Even happier.

'Is your phone okay?'

'No.' The word came out as a growl. 'The screen's broken.'

'Oh, no… I'm so sorry. I didn't mean to

land on you like that, honestly. I got shoved as well.'

Euan was finding it impossible to look away and he could feel his forehead creasing into a frown. 'What are you?' he asked. 'American?'

'No.' The smile widened. 'You're way off. Wrong side of the world, even. I'm a Kiwi.' She tilted her head to look past him and then raised an eyebrow. 'Queue's moving. If you leave a gap, someone else might try and push in and I think there are a few people around here who might be grumpy enough already.' She was shaking her head sadly. 'I really don't understand it.'

Having to take a step closer to the cashier meant that Euan had to look away and he had no intention of looking back. Or of continuing this conversation with a complete stranger. He could still hear her voice behind him, however, and he knew perfectly well that she wasn't speaking to anyone else.

'I mean, it's *Christmas*… How can anyone be so grumpy when it's the most exciting time of the year? I *love* Christmas. And it's *snowing*…'

Okay, the sheer joy in her voice was threatening to tip him over the brink. Euan turned his head. 'And you think that's a *good* thing?'

Those blue, blue eyes widened. 'It's going to be a white Christmas. I've dreamed of having one ever since I was a little kid. We might have Christmas in summer in New Zealand, but we all know a *real* Christmas has snow. And holly with red berries and robins and mistletoe and—'

'And people who are freezing because they can't afford to heat their houses and roads that become inaccessible because of the snow, which can mean that people who get sick or have an accident might actually die before help can arrive.'

The woman's jaw dropped. 'Wow…and I thought the taxi driver was enough of a Grinch. Phew…' She gave her head a tiny shake, which made that tumble of golden curls shimmer under the bright, overhead lighting. 'Is it a Scottish thing to hate Christmas in general or just a white one in particular?'

For a crazy moment, Euan was almost tempted to tell this stranger exactly why Christmas was overwhelmingly difficult for him, on a purely personal basis that had nothing to do with his nationality or the weather.

But, even if she wanted to listen, which was highly unlikely given how it might tarnish that glow of happiness, these were things he never said aloud. To anyone. He did his best not to even think about them. That he'd been pushed too close to that locked place he managed to avoid for the vast majority of the year created a knee jerk defensive reaction.

'Christmas is nothing more than a charade,' he snapped. 'It's fake. As far as I'm concerned it's a promise that life is full of good things when, in reality, that promise gets broken far more often than not. The expectation that kids are going to get everything their hearts desire, that families are going to have a wonderful time cooped up together, that there'll be a feast on every table or maybe even that there's going to be some damned miracle that will suddenly make life perfect, well…'

Well…life's not like that, is it? And, making the most of every Christmas because it might well be the last for someone you love more than anyone else on earth is nothing but a recipe for heartbreak that will haunt you for the rest of your life and be at its worst every single time that one day of the year is approaching…

Not that he said that out loud, of course. Good grief…where was this all coming from, anyway? Euan had never bothered analysing exactly why he still dreaded Christmas so much because that was nothing more than a key to open that locked place where disturbing emotional stuff got relegated. Maybe his cracked phone had been the last straw. Or, more likely, that stupid elf headband. Whatever the cause, he was appalled by the fact that he was dumping it all on a happy tourist who had every right to enjoy her Christmas as much as she wanted to.

'Sorry,' he muttered, turning back to find he had a space in front of him again. That he could actually get close enough to ask to speak to the pharmacist who would have his prescription for controlled drugs ready for him to sign out. He flicked a glance over his shoulder and even managed an apologetic half smile.

'Have a great Christmas,' he added. 'Take no notice of me.'

Take no notice?
As if…
Abby might have been getting a totally

unexpected lecture about the dark side of Christmas, but that accent was *gorgeous*.

This man might win the prize for being the biggest Grinch she'd ever met in her life, but he was also…undeniably gorgeous.

Tall. Not traditionally handsome, perhaps, but he had an astonishingly compelling face. His eyes were as grey as storm clouds about to break and his features were certainly not soft. He was craggy, that was the word. Interesting. It was impossible not to notice those deep lines from his nose to the corners of his mouth and around his eyes when he frowned. And he looked as if he might frown rather a lot, in fact, but even this man's grumpiness was kind of sexy. Imagine if someone could make him smile? That reluctant tilt of his lips as he'd wished her a happy Christmas, just before he'd walked off gave Abby the feeling that a real smile would melt her on the spot.

Not that she'd ever find out. She was watching the Grinch as he got to the counter, only realising now that he didn't appear to have anything in his hands to pay for. He spoke to the cashier, who nodded and pointed him towards a hatch that opened to the prescription part of the pharmacy. A nod then summoned Abby to the counter. She began emptying the numerous items from her basket, starting with the elf headband that was on top.

Okay, it was a ridiculous accessory, especially for an adult to wear. For someone who hated Christmas as much as the intriguing man she'd just encountered, it was probably symbolic of everything that was wrong about Christmas, like hyped-up expectations and promises that got broken. Outrageous enough to be like a red rag to a bull, even. As she was a naturally empathetic person, it took some effort to push aside a curious voice in the back of her mind that was asking why he might feel so strongly about the season. What could have happened that was so awful?

Abby managed to silence the voice by the counter argument that no reason could be enough to justify spoiling the happiness of other people. Especially children. Most especially the kind of sick children that needed every extra bit of joy that came their way. The kind of children that Abby was lucky enough to be about to spend her Christmas with. And…and it was going to be a *white* Christmas. Abby beamed at the cashier as she handed over the headband. As soon as it was rung up, she took the price sticker off it and put it on her head, over her hat.

She looked sideways as she continued unloading her basket, rather hoping that that Grinch would notice what felt rather like an act of defiance. A public affirmation that, even if it made her look silly, she was going to spread as much joy as she could in the next few days. But the man wasn't at the hatch any longer. She could only see his back, as he walked out of the pharmacy with a paper carrier bag in his hand.

It was still early afternoon by the time Abby drove out of Inverness and headed north to the village of Kirkwood. Her sat nav had estimated the journey time at forty minutes but it was clearly going to take longer because daylight seemed to be fading already and it was gloomy enough to make the whirling snowflakes look like glitter in her headlights, which was distracting enough to make unfamiliar, winding roads quite a challenge.

Abby was more than up for the challenge. Growing up on a high-country New Zealand farm and learning to drive through rocky rivers and steep gullies, she had the skills to cope with anything so she was actually enjoying this. Having to focus was a bonus, because she could forget about the fact that the only two people she'd spoken to since she arrived in Scotland had been determined to rain on her Christmas parade. At least she could be sure that nobody like that would be a part of where she was heading.

This Margaret McKendry, the woman who owned the amazing castle, had to be as much of a fan of Christmas as Abby was, to go to what had to be an enormous effort to create something so special for sick children. A Christmas fairy, in fact, who was waving her wand to make a dream come true and provide joyous moments to people who deserved them more than most.

A large Christmas tree was lit up in the central square of Kirkwood village, there were decorations hanging over the streets and the shops looked busy. The snow was falling much more slowly by the time Abby was through the village and, while surfaces like hedges and footpaths were smudged and white, the roads were still clear enough to be safe. A helpful sign told her she was taking the correct turn off to get to Ravenswood Castle and, only minutes later, Abby found her breath completely stolen away as she got her first glimpse of the castle's turrets at the end of a long, treelined driveway. It was dark enough for it to be no more than a silhouette, but as she drove closer lights from many windows twinkled through softly drifting snowflakes and, when she got close enough for the stone walls to be towering above her, Abby could see fairy lights around the arch shaped windows and framing the rather intimidatingly grand main entrance.

She was holding her breath as she climbed the steps and lifted the lion's head knocker to tap on the massive, wooden door. She had a smile on her face, ready to greet the person who opened the door. A butler, perhaps? Or a housekeeper? Maybe it would be Mrs McKendry herself? Abby's smile widened as the door slowly swung open. She couldn't wait to tell anyone she met how excited she was to be here.

A heartbeat later, however, that smile was fading from her face so fast it was gone by the time Abby could take a new breath.

'I don't believe this,' she said. 'What the hell are *you* doing *here*?'

'I could ask you the same thing,' the Grinch said. 'Except I might do it a tad more politely.'

'Who is it, Euan?' The voice from further behind the door was coming closer. 'Oh, I do hope it's our other doctor. She's due to arrive about now and I can't wait to meet her.' The door was pulled from the man's hand. 'Oh, for heaven's sake, don't leave the poor girl standing out in the snow.'

The woman was tiny. No more than five feet tall and she had a pixie cut of pure, white hair over a well-wrinkled face, but the first impression was not one of frailty—quite the opposite.

'I'm Margaret McKendry,' the woman said. 'But please call me Maggie.' Her smile was so welcoming Abby felt as if she were turning up at her own grandmother's house. 'You must be Abby. You're just how I imagined you'd look after we spoke on the phone.'

'Abby Hawkins.' She nodded. 'And I'm so happy to meet you, Maggie.'

'Come in, come in.' Maggie kept talking as Abby stepped inside, coming uncomfortably close to the man she knew was glaring at her. 'We've got a fire going in the drawing room and we'll get you something to eat. Are your keys still in your car?'

'Yes. I've got some bags to get out of the back.'

'Euan can park your car,' Maggie said. 'He'll get your bags and take them up to your bedroom.' She turned to the Grinch. 'I'm putting Abby in the blue room, next to you.'

He actually closed his eyes, Abby noticed, and let out a slow breath, as though he was trying to keep his temper? Or maybe preparing himself to face something unimaginably unpleasant. It was only then that she remembered she was still wearing the silly elf headband. Embarrassed, she snatched it off, but it was clearly too late to appease him in any way. For the second time in little more than an hour, he was turning to walk away from her.

Except he wasn't going to disappear this time, was he? Abby turned back to Maggie and the question in her eyes must have been obvious.

'Oh, I'm sorry, pet.' Maggie stepped forward to push the enormous door shut. 'I didn't introduce you properly. That's Euan, my grandson. He's also the other doctor who's here to care for the children.'

Was it her imagination or was there a gleam of mischief in the older woman's glance as she led Abby across the elaborately tiled floor of an enormous foyer? Her eyes widened as she walked past a trio of what looked like genuine suits of medieval armour. Maggie led her through open double doors into a long, wide room that was filled with light and warmth. A tall Christmas tree stood to one side of an open fireplace wreathed in twinkling lights and covered in a bright rainbow of decorations but Abby wasn't distracted this time. Maggie didn't catch her gaze as she kept walking towards several couches arranged in front of the roaring fire.

She smiled as she sat down, her hand gesture an invitation for Abby to follow suit. 'Don't be fooled by that grumpiness,' she said. 'My Euan's got a heart of gold and I'm sure the two of you will get along like a house on fire.' The tone of her voice was perfectly serene but Abby was suddenly quite sure that Maggie was aware of a lot more than she was letting on.

Like a house on fire might be an apt simile, Abby thought, her heart sinking along with her body as she sat down on the squashy, feather-filled cushions of the couch opposite Maggie. A catastrophic house fire, perhaps, where there was the very real possibility that someone might not survive?

Abby had the horrible feeling that what might not survive was going to be the magical Christmas experience she had been so excited to be a part of. She might have to work very hard—for everybody, including herself—to make sure it was not going to be ruined by a real life Grinch.

At least Maggie was adorable and Abby had no doubt that she'd be on her side of the creating Christmas joy equation. She smiled back at the Grinch's grandmother.

'Don't worry,' she said. 'I've had experience with grumpy men before so I know not to take it personally. You never know, he might find himself enjoying Christmas whether he likes it or not.'

CHAPTER TWO

IT BEGGARED BELIEF, that was what it did.

Euan McKendry climbed the majestically sweeping staircase that led from the main entrance foyer to the first floor of this wing where there were some of the nicest bedrooms in Ravenswood Castle. They all had en suite bathrooms, some had sitting rooms or walk-in wardrobes and one of them—his—had a round wall where it fitted inside one of the larger front turrets of this extraordinary dwelling that dated back to the seventeenth century.

He was carrying a small suitcase in one hand and a large carrier bag in the other. A bag that was heavy enough to have made him glance at the contents to spot toiletries like bottles of shampoo and conditioner. So now, he was off to deposit these belongings in the bedroom that was next door to his turret room and he had a mental image of Dr Abby Hawkins standing in her shower washing that impressive mane of blonde waves. Naked. With soap bubbles sliding down her skin. The thought that she would be singing was a growl in his head and he let it become even more annoying. No doubt she would be singing *Christmas* carols…

It wasn't that he hadn't known Maggie had engaged another doctor to help with the camp. She always did and he'd spoken to his grandmother only a few days ago to hear how thrilled she was with the latest response to her annual advertisement in a prestigious medical journal.

'This one is perfect. The best I've ever found, I think. A paediatrician who's just finished postgraduate training in congenital heart disease, would you believe?'

Right now, Euan would believe anything. If someone had told him in that pharmacy that the Christmas angel come to life who'd almost knocked him over would be landing on his doorstep straight after he'd arrived at his childhood home, he would have laughed it off by saying something like, *Och aye, and pigs might fly.* But, if he'd had any idea at all that she was going to be participating in one of Maggie's fantasy holidays for sick kids, he would never have dreamed of unleashing his opinions about the seasonal festivities. Because Gammy had more than enough to worry about at the moment and the absolute last thing Euan would want was for her to have her heart broken by hearing how much he hated this time of year.

He opened the door of the blue room to see it had been beautifully prepared for a guest. There were fresh flowers in a vase on the dressing table, a stack of fluffy, clean towels on a chair by the bathroom door and the ornately carved four-poster bed had a corner of the thick duvet turned back invitingly to reveal the classic white linen with beautifully embroidered borders.

Not that he was about to allow himself to imagine that bed being occupied. Or think about what Abby Hawkins might wear to sleep in. Even acknowledging how attractive this young doctor was would probably add an unacceptable level of tension to an already difficult few days. Just her presence in the house had ramped up that tension very noticeably so he needed to talk to her in private as soon as possible. To beg her, if that was what it took, not to pass on a single word of what he'd said about Christmas to anyone, but most especially not to Maggie.

Euan left Abby's bags just inside the room and closed the door again. The lighting in this wide hallway came from pairs of glass lamps shaped like flames on long metal torch handles that crossed. A soft light that threw shadows on the heavily framed portraits of bygone generations and made the polish on dark floorboards gleam on either side of the carpet runner. As he walked back to the main staircase, one side of the hallway became a balustrade between pillars that provided a stunning view of the staircase and the foyer below. He could see the open doors of the drawing room as he headed down and knew that was where Abby would be but, for a heartbeat, any plan he was forming to find an excuse to speak to her alone was sabotaged by the kind of ghost that always lay in wait for him here.

He actually turned his head and looked up, as if he could see the small face, peering through the rails of the balustrade, watching him. Waiting for him to go up and read that favourite bedtime story for the umpteenth time, already overjoyed by the prospect. Such a delicate little face with those wispy golden red curls and blue eyes the colour of new denim jeans. A smile that could light up an entire room, even as big as some of the rooms in this castle.

Fiona.

The little sister who'd come into his life when he was seven years old, just weeks after his father had died, which could have contributed to the fierce need to protect her that he'd had from that first captivating moment he'd seen her, along with a love that was so big he'd been sure it could conquer anything. That he'd always be able to keep her safe. He could step into his father's shoes and take care of his whole family. Grandmother, mother and now this precious baby.

The lump in his throat was all too familiar as Euan blinked away the ghost. He knew that he could swallow it, but he also knew that it would sit in his gut and be joined by others to create a weight heavy enough to be physically as well as emotionally painful. It was the same every year but it was going to be worse this time because there was no getting away from the worry about his grandmother's health. That he might have to face up to the reality of losing the last member of his family sooner, rather than later.

He couldn't allow her to be upset by Abby saying anything. This had to be the best year ever. Because it was not only for Fiona, the camp had been the heart and soul of Maggie's life for the last twenty-five years and, while Euan might have been totally unable to protect his family the way he'd wanted to, that love for three generations of McKendry women had never faded.

The glow of happiness he could see on Maggie's face when he entered the drawing room gave his heart a squeeze so tight he had to catch his breath.

'You'll never guess what Abby's just told me,' she said.

'Ahh...' She certainly wouldn't be looking this happy if Abby had told her what Euan was desperately hoping she would keep to herself. 'Nope. I give up. I can't guess.'

'She grew up on a farm. She can drive a tractor and she just told me that using a chainsaw is one of her splinter skills.' Maggie's glance towards Abby was full of admiration. 'You'll have to do the Christmas tree hunt together. Abby's going to be such a great role model for our girls.'

Euan headed for an empty couch. 'Somehow that doesn't surprise me.'

'Why not?' Abby was watching him as he sat down.

Because she was too good to be true? Some kind of cross between a Christmas angel and Superwoman? Euan shrugged rather than admit that out loud. 'Maybe we expect people from Australia and New Zealand to be good at anything to do with the land.'

'Oh…like we expect every Scotsman to be good at playing the bagpipes?'

Maggie laughed. 'Euan *is* very good at playing the bagpipes, as it happens. Wait till you hear some of the Christmas carols he plays up on the ramparts.'

Abby's eyes were dancing. 'Does he wear a kilt, too?'

'But of course.'

'I can't wait.' Abby was grinning now. 'Christmas carols are one of my favourite things.'

The mischievous look she was giving Euan made him wonder what she was about to say concerning men in kilts but, instead, she sighed happily. '"The Little Drummer Boy" is one of the carols I love the most.'

'Not in my current repertoire,' Euan said. 'Sorry.'

'Perhaps you could dust it off,' Maggie suggested. 'It's one of my favourites too. Now... I've asked Catherine to bring us some afternoon tea but do either of you need a rest before we get busy? I'd like us to have a chat about all the children we're expecting to arrive tomorrow and go over our timetable so it might take a wee while.'

'I'm fine,' Abby said. 'I can't wait to get started and I had a bit of a break in Inverness.'

Her face was giving nothing away. And, if she wasn't going to confess she'd already met him in the pharmacy, she probably wasn't about to tell Maggie what he'd said about Christmas being nothing more than a sham and broken promises. The way she was looking as innocent as you'd expect an angel to look made Euan think that she must be very good at keeping secrets and he should be feeling relieved about that but, oddly, it was almost disappointing.

As if she'd dismissed meeting him as too unimportant to bother remembering.

He could feel himself frowning. 'I'm fine too,' he said. 'But what about you, Gammy? Do *you* need a rest?' He knew he was searching her face, looking for any signs of her being in pain or fatigued.

Maggie ignored him, helped by Abby's surprised query.

'*Gammy?*' The word came out with a gurgle of laughter.

Maggie laughed again, too. 'That was Fiona's doing. Euan's wee sister. She couldn't say "Grandma" when she was little so she called me "Gammy". Like a wonky leg. Euan thought it was hilarious, of course—as any nine-year-old would, so he started using it as well.' Maggie shook her head. 'And here he is, a grown man of thirty-six and he's still using it.'

'It's adorable.'

Euan was on the receiving end of that mischievous look again. Combined with the tilt of Abby's lips it felt as if he was being teased. Or charmed, perhaps? It was a relief when Catherine the cook came into the room, wheeling a tea trolley.

'I've got you some of my best shortbread,' she announced after greeting Abby with a smile. 'And mince pies and teatime scones with jam and cream. You'll no' go hungry here, lassie, not while I'm in charge of our kitchens. Coffee or tea?'

'Tea would be wonderful, thank you. And that shortbread looks amazing.' It seemed to be a big decision whether to choose a Christmas tree shaped biscuit or a star. She chose the star. 'Very Christmassy.'

Maggie accepted a proffered cup. 'I do believe we've found someone who loves Christmas as much as I do, Cath.'

'I find that hard to believe.' The cook shook her head but she was smiling. 'But then, we all love Christmas here.' She handed Euan a cup. 'It's good to see you back again, laddie.'

'It's good to be here, Cath,' Euan said. He could feel Abby's gaze on him and he knew what she was thinking—that this castle was about to put on a Yuletide extravaganza that was everything he'd told Abby he deplored about Christmas. But he knew his words would sound genuine because they *were*. Never mind how he felt about Christmas or the responsibility of caring for sick children, he was back in a part of the world he loved the most, with the person he loved the most.

He was home, that was what it was.

And, no matter how difficult it might be, home was the place you were meant to be for Christmas.

They didn't know, did they?

Did nobody here know how much Euan

McKendry hated Christmas? It made Abby feel a little uncomfortable but it was hardly her place to spill a secret like this. Especially not in front of the man's grandmother, who clearly doted on him. Even the castle cook was obviously very fond of this 'laddie' and Abby wasn't about to upset a woman who had a supply of the best, melt-in-the-mouth shortbread she'd ever tasted in her life.

When the afternoon tea trolley had been taken out, Maggie produced document folders that she handed to both Euan and Abby.

'Let's have a quick look at the medical records for the children coming this year first,' she suggested. 'I know you and Abby will need to discuss the medical side of things between yourselves but it would be helpful if you could flag anything that stands out in the way of any more supplies I might need to order in the next few days before the Christmas shut down. Like extra oxygen?'

Euan was nodding as he opened the folder and then Abby saw him smile for the first time.

'Milo's coming again.'

It was a real smile. And Abby had been right to imagine the effect it might have on her. The way it changed and softened his face did make her melt inside. She could feel the tingle right down to the tips of her toes and it was impossible to look away.

'Isn't it wonderful?' Maggie was beaming again. 'It wouldn't really feel like Christmas without Milo here, would it?' She turned to Abby. 'This is his third Christmas at the castle. His mum, Louise, told me they start counting the days right after his birthday in August. He's just the happiest wee boy on the planet. You'll love him as much as we do.'

Having managed to look away from Euan to listen to Maggie, Abby opened her folder to stop her gaze going straight back to him. The first set of medical records in the file told her that Milo was a six-year-old boy with Down's syndrome and he'd been born with a partial atrioventricular septal defect and an abnormality of his aortic valve.

'Surgery to repair the AVSD at eighteen months old,' she murmured as she speed-read. 'With what looks like a few complications post-surgery.'

'He had a tough time.' Euan's tone was neutral. 'And more surgery, including a mitral valve replacement at three years old. The latest procedure was a balloon dilation last year when his aortic stenosis became symptomatic. He was also given up for adoption at birth because the parents turned their backs on what they deemed to be a "defective" child.'

'Oh…that poor baby…' Abby was appalled. 'I can't believe there are still people like that in the world.'

'Fortunately, there are the people who *aren't* like that,' Maggie said quietly. 'And Louise is one of them. She was still single at forty and knew her chances of having a baby were disappearing fast. She was overjoyed to be allowed to adopt Milo and she's been totally devoted to him ever since. She's an expert in baby sign language, which is Milo's main form of communication. And she's coming with him to camp, of course.'

'I'll look forward to meeting them.' Maybe Milo would be a fan of the elf headband that was lying on the couch beside her. 'I've been trying to learn a bit of baby sign language myself in the last few months.'

'We'll talk about his management later,' Euan said. 'I see there's a note about a recent episode of him being short of breath. With his history of aortic stenosis, we'll need to keep an eye on him.'

Euan was already turning a page to the

next set of notes but Abby's brain had briefly veered off on a tangent. There was a dedicated clinic somewhere in the castle and she was going to be working closely with this man for the next few days. What was that going to be like, she wondered, given that she could still feel the odd tingle that had reached her toes when she'd seen him smile?

He really was a seriously attractive man.

Apart from hating Christmas but, in a weird way, that made him even more attractive. Because he was totally different from any man Abby had ever been interested in in the past. Perhaps even a polar opposite of herself? Was this like the way 'bad' boys were so attractive to the girls who would never dream of breaking any rules?

'Leah's our oldest camper this year.' Maggie's voice brought Abby smartly back to the job at hand. 'She's twelve years old and is just over a year past her heart transplant for HLHS. She was chosen for the camp because she needs to build some confidence.'

'I can imagine…' Euan was shaking his head as he scanned the file. 'She's spent a lot of her life in hospital, hasn't she? Multiple arrests and having to be put on bypass more than once. She's lucky to have made it to a transplant.'

'I've been involved with the treatment of quite a few children with hypoplastic left heart syndrome over the last year,' Abby said. 'Despite the increase in survival rates it's still the most severe and life-threatening form of congenital heart disease.'

'You'll find that the majority of children who are chosen to come to our camps have HLHS,' Maggie told her.

'Oh? Is there a reason for that?'

Instead of answering her, Maggie shifted her gaze to Euan, her eyebrows raised, as if she was inviting him to answer Abby's query. There was a frisson of something in the room that felt tense, as well—as if the explanation was significant—but Euan simply shrugged.

'As you say, hypoplastic left heart syndrome is one of the more challenging forms of CHD. Add in difficult family circumstances and they're the kind of kids the associations put forward for a special treat like our Christmas camps.' He cleared his throat as he turned another page. 'Ben's a good example,' he continued briskly. 'Six years old. He had in-utero surgery to correct an aortic stenosis at twenty-two weeks and four open-heart surgeries for his HLHS by the age of three. He has some developmental delays and difficulty with spatial tasks. His grandmother is coming as his carer because his mother has just had a new baby and there are also older siblings to care for.'

Abby could still feel that tension in the room. Maybe it was the way Maggie was still watching her grandson, her brow furrowed in what looked like concern. Sadness, even? She only looked away when someone came through the doors of the drawing room.

'Sorry to interrupt, Mrs McKendry, but there's a phone call for you. They say it's urgent.'

Maggie got to her feet with a speed and grace that belied her years. 'Thanks, Ruth. I'll come right now.' She looked over her shoulder as she began walking out of the room. 'Ruth's one of our volunteers from the village,' she told Abby. 'She helps with the admin side of the camps. I'll introduce you to everybody later but I'd better take this call, I think. I do hope it's not someone who's too unwell to come to camp.'

For a long moment after Maggie had disappeared, there was such a deep silence that the crackle of flames in the fireplace sounded loud. Abby pretended to be reading the notes on her lap but the words were not sinking in. She was too aware of Euan sitting on the other couch. Was he, too, pretending to read? She sneaked a peek only to find that he was staring at *her* and, to her dismay, Abby could feel heat flooding into her cheeks. She was *blushing*? Maybe she was mortified because that look was making her feel as if she was the last person on earth Euan would want to be looking at.

'What?' she found herself asking. 'Is it a problem that I'm here? Do you need to have a look at my CV to check my qualifications?'

'Of course not. My grandmother is more than capable of choosing the best medical backup to keep the children on her camps as safe as possible.' He closed his eyes as he rubbed his forehead with his fingertips. 'You're just the last person I expected to see here after…you know…the way we met.'

'I bet I was even more surprised,' Abby said. 'When you can't wait to get to a place that sets out to make Christmas as magical as possible, the absolute last person you'd expect to find there is someone who hates everything to do with the season.'

The way Euan's eyes snapped open as he

threw such a swift, almost fearful, glance over his shoulder made Abby bite her lip.

'Don't worry,' she said. 'I'm trying to forget I heard it in the first place so I'm not likely to say anything to anyone else.'

'Thank you,' Euan said slowly. Then he sighed. 'My only excuse for such an inappropriate outburst to a complete stranger is that I'm finding this a somewhat stressful time. Maggie's not going to tell you that she's unwell but she's waiting for some biopsy results on an abdominal growth that could be serious.'

Abby put her hand to her mouth. 'Oh… I had no idea. I'm so sorry to hear that.'

'We might not know before Christmas but that's enough for her to be dealing with and the distraction of the celebrations is probably a good thing so I don't want her to know… ah…about my stress levels.'

'No… I understand.' Which wasn't entirely true. There was more to it, Abby thought, but it really wasn't any of her business, was it? 'Look, I think your gran is an amazing woman with what she's doing for these children and I'm only here to do whatever I can to help in any way. It doesn't have to be simply medical. I'm up for participating in any of the activities.' She smiled at Euan. 'Especially if I get to play with a chainsaw, although…' She turned her head. Up close she could see that the bright array of decorations on the tree beside the fire were tiny toys made of wood, like soldiers and teddy bears and rocking horses. 'This is already a gorgeous Christmas tree. Where's another one going to go?'

'We have the biggest one outside, for when the village children come to the camp's Christmas party. There'll be another one in the foyer and we have little ones in everybody's rooms. Santa leaves a few surprises under those ones during the night.'

Maggie had come back into the room in time to hear his last words.

'Speaking of surprises,' she said, 'it looks like we might have an extra camper coming. A little CHD girl called Lucy and her brother Liam. That was someone from Social Services on the phone—Judith—who had my number because she visited once with another child, a few years ago. She's so upset about the situation these children are in, she's prepared to give up her own Christmas to bring them here as their carer.'

'Have we got room?' Euan was eyeing

the files yet to be opened. 'We seem to have our usual tally of campers already.' The moment's silence in response made him expel his breath in a huff. 'Silly question. Of course we've got room.'

He was smiling again. This time, Abby intercepted the look he was giving Maggie. A look of fond tolerance. Understanding. A bone-deep love that was almost fierce in its intensity. It wasn't just her toes that tingled this time. Abby could feel such a tight squeeze on her heart that it took her breath away. She wondered if Maggie was feeling what she would feel if someone looked at *her* like that.

As if she was the luckiest woman in the world…

CHAPTER THREE

GETTING FAMILIAR WITH the general background of the children they would be caring for this year was the easy bit. Discussing their medical needs in more detail with Abby would not be a problem, either. Euan was quite sure she would be impressed with the extra equipment they had available in the castle's clinic specifically to identify the first signs that a heart was failing to cope with its task of pumping oxygenated blood to the whole body. They had the ability to monitor levels of oxygen saturation in the blood, heart rhythms and rates, blood pressure, and smart, digital scales that could distinguish whether fluid retention was contributing to weight. If a higher degree of assessment was needed, they had a very good relationship with the cardiology department at the main regional hospital in Inverness where cardiac ultrasound equipment was available to check on heart function with an echocardiogram.

What wasn't so easy were all the other bits that had nothing to do with the medical care of these children.

The Christmas stuff.

Euan would have simply excused himself from the room while Abby was becoming progressively more thrilled with the timetable for the next few days except that he'd heard the catch in Maggie's voice when she was starting to tell her more about the camp and the activities that were on offer. She was in pain, he was sure of it.

'You have a petting farm? Oh, wow...'

'It's not huge. A couple of donkeys, who have suitably Christmas names of Joseph and Mary.' Maggie's face lit up. 'Mary's pregnant but donkey foals can take anywhere from eleven to fourteen and a half months to appear so we don't know yet when it will arrive. We have a few bottle-raised sheep as well and a cow. And there are our ancient Clydesdales that are long retired but can pull the sleigh. They wear reindeer antlers that I had specially made to attach to their bridles a very long time ago. Twenty-five years ago, in fact.'

She was avoiding catching Euan's gaze. Because they both knew that those antlers had been made for that very first time there was more than one child with severe heart disease at the castle for Christmas. The year that Fiona's very best friend, Jamie, had come to stay. Four-year-old Fi had actually burst into tears of joy on that sleigh ride. At eleven, Euan had been far too grown-up to cry but he could still remember the way it had felt as if a giant hand had taken hold of his heart and squished it. How happy he'd been to see his beloved baby sister so happy.

Even the echo of that squeeze gave him another one of those lumps that had to be swallowed. It wasn't helping that Abby was looking more and more as though *she* was about to burst into tears of joy. Or that Maggie clearly needed a painkiller. He could see the way her fingers were digging into the upholstery on the arm of the couch.

'Are you all right, Gammy?'

'Never better.' Maggie gave him a bright smile. 'You know I'm never happier than when I've got someone to plan Christmas celebrations with.'

'That's not what I was asking. When did you last have a dose of your medication?'

Maggie's gaze slid instantly away from his. 'With my cup of tea. You were too busy scoffing Cath's shortbread to notice.'

'Has Graham been to check on you today?'

'Why would he? None of the children have arrived yet.' Maggie sent an apologetic glance in Abby's direction. 'Graham's our local GP. He likes to get involved with camp in case we need any backup.'

'To see you,' Euan said. 'Maybe I'll ring and have a word.'

'Don't you go making extra work for him when it's not needed.' Again, it was Abby who was given an explanation. 'He's been trying to retire for years but it's not easy to attract doctors to a little village like Kirkwood. And I'm fine, Euan.'

Her tone was telling him in no uncertain terms that the matter was not up for further discussion. Or maybe it was a warning that it could be taken in another direction—the one where he was disappointing the whole village by choosing to be a GP at pretty much the opposite end of the United Kingdom. It was fair enough if Maggie didn't want to talk about her health concerns in front of Abby. And Euan certainly didn't want to discuss why he'd made his career choices but he was also determined that Maggie was not going to spend the next few days in more pain than she needed to be in. It was more than half an hour since they'd had that afternoon tea so the analgesics should be reaching peak effect soon.

And, while he would much prefer to remove himself from hearing about the kind of frivolous seasonal activities both these women clearly revelled in, he wanted to keep a close eye on his grandmother for a little while longer. He would notice the slightest body language like a grimace or stiffness that could indicate inadequate pain relief and he could talk to Maggie quietly later on and persuade her to try something a bit stronger.

Maggie had turned her attention back to Abby. 'So, we have a lot of indoor activities for the children. You might have noticed already how short our days are this far north. We don't have much more than six hours of daylight at this time of year.'

'I know, it's crazy, isn't it? Here it is not even four o'clock and it looks like the middle of the night out there.'

When Abby swung her head to look towards the wall of arched windows that looked out on the entranceway to the castle, it made the length of her hair ripple as it fell over her shoulder. She was sitting close enough to the fire to be catching the glow of flames and the chandelier above her head seemed to be adding another sparkle to that amazing shade of gold. Euan couldn't take his eyes off her.

'But I love it,' Abby added. 'It makes everything brighter, like the lights on Christmas trees and even the flames in a fire look warmer. And we can wear woolly hats and mittens and have all the wonderful, hot comfort food like roast potatoes and gravy. It never feels quite right when it's bright sunshine and scorchingly hot.'

Euan closed his eyes in a long blink. How good would that be? To spend Christmas Day just lying on a beach and soaking up the sun without a care in the world? So why did listening to Abby talk about a frozen, dark Christmas Day make it seem so damned inviting? As if it were the best thing in the world?

It wasn't.

It was an ordeal that you had to get through every year, for the sake of other people who actually believed that it could somehow create some kind of a miracle. Euan wasn't seeing any signs that Maggie was suffering. Quite the opposite—she was clearly enjoying this discussion with Abby—but it was getting rapidly more annoying for him to sit here and listen. He didn't want to hear about exciting outdoor expeditions to cut down pine trees, build snowmen, or go ice skating on the lake. He was even less interested in the craft sessions to make Christmas decorations or bake Christmas cookies and as for the letter writing session to tell Father Christmas what they were wishing for the most…

Okay, that did it. He *really* had to get out of here. Euan propelled himself to his feet swiftly enough to startle both Maggie and Abby.

'I've got to go.' The words came out in a snap that he knew sounded rude so Euan tried to excuse his abrupt exit. 'There's… ah…'

What? Something he needed to do? Someone to see? Ghosts to escape from? He shook his head, words failing him, so he just lifted his hand by way of farewell and walked away.

He couldn't get away fast enough, could he?

And this was getting ridiculous. Euan

McKendry seemed to have already made it a habit to walk out on her but Abby found her heart sinking again as she watched the way Euan McKendry straightened his back and walked away so decisively this time. She'd been right in thinking that it was going to be hard work not allowing him to dampen the joy of Christmas.

Maggie hadn't been watching her grandson leave the room, however, because Abby found that she was the focus of the older woman's gaze when she turned back.

'I know...' She dug deep to find a cheerful smile. 'He's got a heart of gold. He's just one of those classically grumpy Scotsmen that I'm sure isn't actually a genuine stereotype?'

She expected Maggie to smile back, so they could brush off the effect of Euan's brisk-enough-to-be-rude exit and get back to talking about Christmas but, instead, she was looking almost as if she might be about to cry?

'There's something you should probably know,' she said quietly.

Uh, oh...after many years of being part of often very intense medical situations, Abby knew what it was like to both hear and deliver significant information that could change someone's life. Whatever it was that Maggie was about to tell her was clearly going to change at least the next few days of her own life. She said nothing and just sat very still to listen carefully.

'I thought Euan might say something when you asked why most of the children who come here have HLHS.'

Abby nodded. She remembered that frisson of something tense in the room.

'It's what his wee sister, Fiona, was born with. Just a short time after his daddy had been killed in an accident on the farm. Euan was just a bairn—seven years old.'

'Oh…' Abby caught her lip between her teeth. 'That's tragic…' Had it happened at Christmas time? Was that why Euan hated the season so much?

'Aye…' Maggie pressed a finger to the bridge of her nose and it looked like a well-practised way to stem any unwanted tears. 'But the baby saved Euan from thinking it was the end of the world. I've never seen a child fall in love with a baby like that. He adored her.'

It was already plain to see how much Euan loved his grandma so Abby could easily picture him besotted with a sister so much younger than himself. How precious that little life would have seemed when it was hanging in the balance so soon after losing his dad.

'She was the happiest wee girl,' Maggie said. 'Despite everything she had to go through. Or maybe because of it. And she had so much love to give. It was because she wanted her best friend, Jamie—another heart baby—to visit, that Camp Christmas started in the first place. It grew a bit every year after that.'

Abby knew the statistics. That first camp had been a very long time ago and very few children with such a serious congenital heart condition made it to adulthood but she didn't want to ask any of the questions that were springing to mind, like how old Fiona had been when she died and whose idea had it been to keep the camp running afterwards when it must have been such a sad reminder of their loss?

Maggie obviously saw something in her face because her face softened. 'Ask Euan,' she told her. 'I've no business to be telling a story that's his as much as mine if he doesn't want it to be told. I just wanted you to know enough to understand why he is like he is.'

Her breath came out in a sigh. 'This is a hard time of year for him.'

'I understand,' Abby said softly.

Maggie got to her feet—a clear indication that this conversation was over but a smile on her face to soften the dismissal. 'Let me show you to your room. You'll need time to settle in before dinner and I have some organising to do to get ready for the unexpected addition to our numbers.'

Abby changed her mind a while later, when she'd finished tiptoeing around a room that made her feel as if she'd just stepped between the pages of a fairy tale and become some kind of princess and was getting on with the business of unpacking her clothes and the bag of new toiletries she'd purchased in Inverness. She didn't understand.

Oh, she could understand why Euan hated Christmas, with the sad memories it must invoke, but that didn't explain why he came here, year after year, to take part in a celebration that could only be heart wrenching. Was that for Maggie's sake? Or had it started because he could take care of other sick children when he could no longer care for his beloved sister? Was that why he'd chosen to become a doctor? And why hadn't Maggie said anything about his mother?

It was more than mere curiosity. Abby's heart had been well and truly captured by imagining Euan as a serious, young boy, living here in this astonishing castle, wanting to protect the little sister he adored but being all too aware of the cloud of fear that hung over the whole family. She wanted to hear his story so much it was all she could think about but it had to be his choice to tell her. Forcing him would only be cruel.

About as cruel as the way she'd gone on and on about how much she loved Christmas. By wearing that stupid elf headband. By the way she'd practically labelled Euan as the enemy who was out to stifle any seasonal joy. A Grinch. The more she thought about it, the more it made Abby cringe inside.

She wanted to apologise.

No, it went a lot deeper than that, actually.

What Abby wanted was to try and make Christmas just a little more bearable for Euan McKendry. What a gift that would be, if she could give him even a moment or two of the kind of real joy she always found. It would be a gift for Maggie, as well. One for herself, in fact, because Abby's heart was still aching for that little boy who'd loved his baby sister that much. A young person who'd had to deal with another huge loss in his life probably only a few years down the track. And for the man Euan was now, whose courage was seriously impressive. Okay, so he was trying to protect his own heart by turning his back on the magic of Christmas and hiding behind grumpiness, but here he was, brave enough to be taking part, yet again, in a celebration of the season like none other Abby had ever heard of.

If there was something she could do to make the next few days at least more bearable, if not actually enjoyable, then she would be grabbing the opportunity with both hands.

Why was Abby smiling at him like that?

As if his company, heading outside through the kitchen door at the back of the castle, at nine o'clock, as the sun finally rose above the mountains the next morning, was all that she could have wished for.

Maybe he should have said 'no' to his grandmother's request after breakfast this morning. Except it had been more of an order than a request, hadn't it?

'The first children aren't scheduled to arrive until much later this morning so you've plenty of time,' she'd said.

'For what?'

'I was thinking about what Abby said at dinner last night.'

'What about?' She'd certainly had plenty to say and she'd given no indication that she found Euan's lack of contribution to the conversation annoying. And he had to admit that, not only was she a born storyteller, it had been no hardship to listen to her cute accent.

'Mistletoe. I had no idea it might not grow in New Zealand like it does here. Fancy never having seen it except for a picture on a Christmas card.'

'She hasn't missed much. It's just a parasite. I've never understood why it became associated with kissing.'

'Someone told me it has to do with fertility,' Maggie said. 'Or celebrating life, perhaps. Because it stays green when the trees lose all their leaves in winter so it's very obvious.'

Euan grunted. 'It's not the only strange Christmas tradition, I suppose. I wonder how many people used to break teeth on the silver coins that went into the plum pudding?'

Maggie wagged her finger at him. 'Don't try and change the subject. I told Abby I need some mistletoe for decorations and that you'd take her to find it. She's in the boot room finding some wellies her size.'

'I'm sure Duncan has far more idea of where to look—it's not as though it's a common thing up here. I've got a lot to do, Gammy. I want to make sure we're well stocked in the clinic.'

'Duncan's gone into Inverness to get replacement bulbs for some of the outdoor lighting. The effect of the sleigh moving up on the ramparts will be ruined with that gap in the sequence.' Maggie was all but pushing Euan in the direction of the boot room that lay between the kitchen and laundry areas at the back of the ground floor. 'I know exactly where some is growing. Do you remember that old, old apple tree that's beside the lake? Near where the rowboat is?'

So, here they were, their waterproof boots leaving deep footprints in the pristine snow of the paths that led through the kitchen gardens and then across a wide expanse of lawn to approach the edge of the forest.

And Abby was smiling at him.

A moment later, however, she had stopped

dead in her tracks with a gasp and she clutched his arm with her hand.

'*Oh...*'

The sound came out with a cloud of mist from Abby's breath, which Euan found himself watching as if he'd never seen the phenomenon before. He was also aware of how acutely he could feel the touch of her hand on his arm, despite the layers of his woolly jumper and puffer jacket and her thick, woollen gloves.

'*Look...*' The instruction came with another cloud of mist.

Euan had to shade his eyes against the shafts of sunlight now filtering through tree tops to the edges of the forest in deep shade and it took a slight movement to see what had caught Abby's attention so completely. It was a small group of fallow deer, just standing at the moment, staring back at the humans disturbing their morning. The buck had a magnificent set of antlers and the hinds were just waiting for his signal before they turned and vanished into the forest with a flick of the black stripe surrounded by white on their tails.

'Did you *see* that?'

'Aye...' Euan found himself smiling. Who

wouldn't, hearing the sheer joy in Abby's voice?

'I mean, it's not as if I haven't seen wild deer in the back country in New Zealand but…this is Scotland and there's a gorgeous forest and…and so much snow. And it's *Christmas* and…'

Abby stopped abruptly, biting her lip as her face suddenly changed to look, what… something beyond apologetic, perhaps?

'I'm annoying, aren't I? Sorry. I promise I won't say the "C" word again for…ooh, at least five minutes?'

Her expression was changing again, morphing into the kind of amused teasing he'd seen when Abby had learned that he called his grandmother 'Gammy'.

And he'd been correct in thinking that it was also charming. Her joy in things like Christmas and the snow and spotting wild deer was equally charming, even if it could be deemed somewhat childish. And…well… it was distracting, wasn't it?

For a little while, at least, it was making it noticeably easier to forget about that dark, sad cloud that was always ready to roll in when he was here at this time of year and that it was so much darker this year, what with Maggie's impending diagnosis hanging over them. Not only that, when Euan had opened his emails before breakfast this morning, he'd found information on the unexpected additional child who was about to arrive. The five-year-old girl, Lucy, wasn't simply a congenital heart disease patient. She had HLHS, like Fiona. It wasn't just a brother who was coming with her, either, but a big brother, Liam, who was ten years old. How could Euan be around these two children without seeing a potential mirror image of himself as a lad and Fiona when she had been the same age, which was probably her healthiest and happiest time ever? When life had held a promise he had actually started believing in. When he'd looked forward to Christmas as much as anyone else.

Euan led Abby along a forest path he'd been using ever since he could walk. There was sunlight reaching through the bare branches of the huge, ancient oak trees but it wasn't providing any warmth yet. A cheeky robin fluttered nearby and Euan knew, even before he slid a sideways glance at Abby, that she would be entranced all over again. As if she felt the glance, she turned her head and yes…her face was lit up with delight but she had her lips firmly pressed together so that she remained silent.

He almost chuckled out loud but, instead, followed Abby's example and pressed his own lips firmly enough together to prevent even a smile escaping. The fact that he actually had the urge to smile or laugh was distracting in itself. More than that, it seemed to have released some endorphins or something. Euan actually had a moment of feeling better than he had in quite some time. Who would have thought…?

It was obvious that Abby was making an effort to find something to talk about other than Christmas.

'So, I meant to ask…are you a specialist paediatrician? Or cardiologist?'

'No.' They were specialties Euan would never have considered devoting his career to. How much heartbreak would there be in spending your life working with families who were going through the kind of challenges he knew only too well? 'I'm just a GP,' he told Abby.

'It's never "just" a GP,' Abby said. 'There's an enormous responsibility in being the first person to pick up significant problems and manage them with appropriate referrals.

Then there's the day-to-day management that comes back to you. You must need to dip into every specialty there is depending on the needs of your patients.'

Euan grunted. It was true. Amidst all the ordinary, and sometimes repetitively dull, tasks in general practice, there was the satisfaction of the detective work and the stimulation of acquiring new knowledge and skills.

'I might well end up being a GP myself,' Abby told him.

'Have you not already lined up a specialist hospital consultancy after the training you've just done? Back in New Zealand or here in the UK?'

Abby shook her head. 'I'm thirty-two. The career decisions I make now will probably determine what I do for the rest of my life so I decided I would take my time to be very sure of exactly what it is I want for my future.'

'But you must love working with children, yes?'

'Oh, yes...' Abby's smile was confirmation of the joy her work provided. 'In fact, that's the one thing I can be absolutely sure of. I want children in my life. And not just professionally, which is why a job as a GP could be perfect. Or maybe as a consultant part time, I guess. They're the kind of positions that would work well when I've got a few kids.'

Euan blinked. 'How many is "a few"?'

'At least six.' Abby was grinning now. 'I was an only child. Wonderful parents but nothing really got rid of that loneliness. When I played with my dolls or stuffed animals, I always gave them brothers and sisters. Even when I played with the button jar, I made families with a couple of big buttons and lots of little ones.'

Dear God, Abby was a nightmare. Exactly the sort of woman that Euan avoided at all costs. He had, in fact, politely ended more than one relationship in the past when he learned that a girlfriend saw motherhood as a priority in her future. Having his own child was even less appealing than becoming a paediatric cardiologist would have been. So why did imagining her as a small child, sorting buttons into families, make him want to smile again?

He could feel his scowl deepening. 'I suppose it's just as well there are people like you in the world,' he muttered. 'The human race would become extinct if everybody felt like I do about having children.'

At least they'd reached the halfway point of this expedition. In a few minutes, they could start heading back to the castle. Euan could see the old wooden rowboat that hadn't been used for years but hadn't been taken away because it looked so picturesque floating on the end of its long rope. Not that it was floating currently because it looked to be firmly wedged in the ice of Ravenswood estate's frozen lake. Abby was heading straight for the lake edge, looking as if she intended to try ice skating in her wellies.

'Careful,' Euan warned. 'I haven't checked it yet. It might look solid but it can have weaker spots, especially near the edges.'

'Isn't ice skating one of the activities available for the camp kids?'

'Aye. But that depends on what the ice is like. I'll make sure it's safe and mark any dodgy areas with safety cones. It's a very gentle ice-skating experience, anyway. Most of the kids aren't up for any strenuous activities.'

'Do you have ice skates for big people, too?'

Oh, man… That shine in those astonishingly blue eyes. You'd want to say 'yes' to anything, wouldn't you?

Euan just grunted instead. 'Let's get on with what we're here for. See that tree over there?'

'The really scraggly one? With the weird green birds' nests?'

'Aye. Those weird green birds' nests are the mistletoe.'

'No way... I thought they grew in, you know...circles.'

Euan could feel his face shifting into an expression of disbelief but then he saw the amusement dancing in Abby's eyes. Of course she didn't think the plant grew naturally in the kind of wreaths she'd seen on Christmas cards. This time, having unexpectedly fallen for the teasing, it was even harder to stop himself smiling. He could feel his lips twitching as he walked towards the tree.

'I'll do the climbing,' he told her. 'I started climbing this particular tree to get the apples when I was a wee lad so I know what I'm doing.' His sideways glance was deadpan. 'Trust me, I'm a doctor.'

It was working. Sort of.

He'd almost smiled properly that time.

Trying to win Euan McKendry's friendship as a first step to changing his negative view of Christmas was actually adding to Abby's enjoyment of her first morning at Ravenswood Castle. Waking up in the downy warmth of that amazing bed and then getting up to a delicious full English breakfast provided by Catherine the cook had been wonderful but what had come next was so much better. The icy chill of this morning air, the gorgeous deep snow, the spectacular red glow of the rising sun and the joy of seeing both the deer and that cute little robin. They would have been enough of a pleasure all on their own but watching Euan thaw even a tiny bit was giving her an internal warmth that was just delicious.

He might still have his protective barriers well in place but Abby intended to keep tapping until she found a weak spot—a bit like the way Euan probably tested the ice on this lake—and then she could put enough careful pressure on it to get through without causing any harm. Hopefully, with an invitation, even.

That was the plan, anyway.

She was learning more about him in the meantime. Realising that they were polar opposites in more ways than how they felt about Christmas. Abby couldn't imagine not wanting to have children. Although she was still totally focused on a career she was passionate about and loving the freedom to add adventure into her life like the extraordinary Christmas she was about to experience this year, becoming a mother was, in fact, the number one priority in her future.

Not that she was thinking about that right now, as she watched Euan climb into this gnarly old apple tree. She was watching the graceful movement of his body and the obvious strength in his arms as he pulled himself up, the focused expression on his face and then the delicate way he detached the rounded mass of greenery without damaging the branches that forked around it. Part of her brain was smudging what she was watching, apparently giving her the ability to time travel and see a small boy climbing this tree instead.

A happy kid who had no idea of what life was going to throw at him in the future or that it would hurt him enough to make him step back from living it to the full. Not even wanting a family of his own, even though he was having to face the prospect of possibly losing his grandmother in the near future. For a moment, Abby felt so sad that if the freezing temperatures hadn't been enough, her eyes would have been stinging anyway. She rubbed at her nose with her glove, suspecting it was both red and drippy.

'Here…catch, Abby.'

But the mistletoe didn't quite make it into her waiting hands because it snagged on some lower, outer branches. They were just a few inches too high for Abby to reach, even standing on tiptoes.

'I'll find a stick.'

'I can reach it. I'll just get this smaller one before I come down. Maggie's bound to have plans that need more than one weird bird's nest.'

Abby hadn't moved by the time Euan shimmied down from the tree only a minute later, with a smaller ball of mistletoe in his hands. His nose and cheeks were reddened by both the physical effort and the cold and he was breathing hard.

'You look like a dragon,' Abby told him. 'Puffing steam.'

'Hmph.'

She was getting used to that grunt that was clearly an important part of Euan's vocabu-

lary. He reached over her head to unsnag the
first mistletoe he'd harvested and, as it began
to fall, Abby also reached up, to catch it. So
she was looking up, with her arms above
her head, as Euan looked down to see where
the ball had gone. He was much closer than
Abby had realised. So close that…

…that the moment suddenly froze.

She couldn't move. Euan seemed to be as
still as she was. It was a blink of time but
more than long enough for something to click
into place.

It wasn't conscious. It had to be the result of a lot of things. Things like how excited Abby was to be here, in this spectacular
place. The way Euan's story had captured
her heart so firmly and her determination
to try and do something to help him. The
fact that, despite his outward grumpiness and
the impression he wasn't that happy to have
her here, there was a level of attraction that
was the final catalyst for what Abby realised
might be the perfect way to make this Christmas more enjoyable for this man.

She hadn't lowered the mistletoe and that
was the perfect excuse for what she did next.

Abby stood on her tiptoes and kissed him.
She'd only intended it to be a friendly sort

of kiss. A brief, under-the-mistletoe, Christmassy sort of kiss. One that wasn't going to be significant in any way.

But the instant her lips touched his, everything changed…

CHAPTER FOUR

IT WAS KIND of like walking along a beach, just a little too close to the waves. For most of the time, the sea was just the background to your walk on the sand, but every so often one of the waves would be a bit bigger and would flow over your feet and, for a moment, all you could think about was that wash of cool water and your connection to the mind-blowing depths and width of the ocean beside you.

Being in the castle clinic, for a medical meet and greet of all the children and their carers arriving for Camp Christmas, with Euan in the main consulting room and Abby in the treatment room of the converted stable block, was kind of like the walk on the sand. The waves that he couldn't stop rolling too close to his feet at random intervals were the memories of that kiss.

Holy moly...*that* kiss.

That totally unexpected, uninvited, kiss that had been like nothing Euan McKendry had ever experienced in his entire life. The touch of Abby's lips on his own had been as if that extraordinary glow that shone around Abby Hawkins had been condensed into an energy and heat that was being directly transferred from one human to another.

From Abby to himself.

Sparks to a source of tinder-dry fuel he hadn't known existed within his mind and body. Or was it an alchemy of a mix of unknown chemistry that had produced something hitherto not even in existence for anyone? Abby seemed to have felt a similar reaction judging by the stunned silence in which they'd walked back to the castle, broken only by a brief, professional discussion about the questions to ask and baseline observations to take as part of the settling in process for the children when they arrived at the castle.

The kind of quick check up Euan was currently doing for Leah, a shy twelve-year-old who was a year past successful heart transplant surgery.

'You'll know the drill.' Euan smiled. 'This

is just a quick check to give us some base-lines so we'll know if anything changes over the next few days. I want to weigh you and have a listen to your lungs and heart. The usual sort of stuff.'

Leah nodded solemnly. So did her father, John, who had come as her carer.

'How are you feeling today?'

'Good.'

'Normal energy level? Appetite?'

Leah nodded. 'I had chips. On the train.'

Euan caught Leah's dad's gaze and he also nodded. 'She's been good,' he said. 'Very excited about coming to the camp. We both are. Leah's a bit nervous, too, mind you. The only holiday away from home that she's had pretty much in her whole life has been to go to hospital.'

'You're going to have the best time,' Euan told her. 'I promise. Come and jump on the scales for me.' He watched how cautiously the girl got up from her chair to walk across the room and then picked up her file to take a note of her weight. But something else on the page caught his attention first.

'No changes in Leah's medication since these notes were sent through?'

'I don't think so. Immunosuppressants, antivirals, the diuretics and that stuff for her stomach… I've forgotten what it's called…'

'Ranitidine,' Euan supplied. 'And there's a magnesium supplement listed here as well.'

'I've got them all in here.' John held out the plastic container he was holding. 'Sorted into days and times. Enough for well over a week.' His smile was embarrassed. 'I was a bit worried we might get snowed in when I saw the weather forecast.'

'They always manage to keep our roads clear enough to get through,' Euan reassured him. 'We've got a good supply of medications here, too, and the hospital in Inverness is not that far away. Try not to worry. We'll take very good care of Leah.'

Her father's anxiety might be partly why his daughter was lacking confidence, Euan thought. He'd bring that up in the meeting he was due to have with Maggie and Abby later today.

In almost the same moment as her name came into his head, Euan found himself distracted by another potential wash of remembering that kiss. Or maybe it was because he could hear a peal of laughter coming from the treatment room that was only separated from this consulting room by a sliding door that wasn't completely closed. Abby was having the pleasure of greeting Milo and was clearly enjoying meeting him and his mother, Louise, as she took his baseline observations.

It wasn't just the wash of a wave he needed to sidestep as Euan focused on his patient, recording Leah's weight and getting her to sit on the bed so that he could listen to her chest. This time, just for a split second, he was even more aware of the ocean behind the wave and, while he certainly wasn't going to allow himself to even think about it right now, he knew exactly where that enormous volume of water slotted into the simile he'd come up with. If the waves represented merely a kiss, the ocean was the unknown enormity of what *more* than kissing Abby Hawkins would be like. And, despite an obvious risk of drowning, Euan knew that the temptation would no doubt be totally irresistible. She might have initiated that kiss entirely by herself but he hadn't exactly been slow to respond, had he? He'd been lost, in fact, from the moment her lips touched his.

Through the disc of his stethoscope, he could hear the healthy *lub-dub*, *lub-dub* of a heart that was working perfectly well, its rate and rhythm within normal parameters.

'Sounds great,' he told Leah. 'I'm going to take your blood pressure now and then you and Dad can go and finish unpacking and explore the castle. I believe lunch is a bit of a picnic in the kitchens so you can go and meet Cath and all her helpers whenever you're ready. Are you going to come out to the pine forest this afternoon to watch us cut down the big Christmas tree?'

Leah shook her head. 'It's really snowy out there,' she said. 'It's hard to walk and… and I might fall over.'

Euan kept his tone casual. 'That's a shame. We've got a doctor here who's helping me look after everybody and she's a girl. Dr Abby, her name is, and do you know, she's the one who's going to cut down that tree? With a *chainsaw*. Don't know about you, but I can't wait to see that.'

Leah and her father had matching expressions of disbelief on their faces.

'I'll walk right beside you, if you like,' he offered, as he wrapped a small cuff around Leah's upper arm to take her blood pressure reading. 'That way I can make sure you don't fall over.'

Even with the earpieces of his stethoscope in place he could still hear the laughter coming from the adjacent room. His patient's new heart might have a pleasingly normal rate and rhythm but he could feel his own skip a beat and speed up at the sound of Abby's laughter. This was another entirely inappropriate time to allow himself to soak in the memory of that kiss but it was easy enough to dodge that wave when needed. Would it be just as easy, Euan wondered, to *not* dodge it? To summon it, even, if he happened to need, say…a bit of distraction?

He'd been distracted earlier today for a moment or two, when Abby's joy in seeing those deer had made him smile. And again, when he'd been trying not to smile because of something she'd said or the expression on her face. Just being around Abby was a distraction all in itself but that kiss had taken it to a completely new level.

It could be useful.

It might even turn out to be a bit of a lifesaver.

From starting out with quiet moments of magic, like seeing the deer as the sun rose to gild a winter wonderland and a kiss that had blown everything Abby Hawkins thought she'd known about kissing right out of the water, her first full day at Ravenswood Castle had spiralled into what could only be described as chaos.

Controlled chaos, for the most part, as people from the village, both employed and volunteers, streamed in to make the final preparations for the arrival of the children and their carers. There was a welcome committee headed by Maggie and excited children and their siblings who were impatient with administrative details like rooms to be allocated and luggage to stow and a check that any special needs were able to be catered for. A team of people helping Catherine the cook was providing refreshments and a rolling picnic style lunch that was being served in the kitchens and dining room. Both Euan and Abby were back and forth to the clinic rooms in the converted stable to match the children to their medical records and start the monitoring that would be routine for the next few days.

Abby was loving every minute of it. These weren't children with congenital heart disease who were sick enough to be admitted to hospital, because their condition had suddenly deteriorated or they were about to undergo major surgery, accompanied by frightened parents who were fearing the worst. These kids had all spent so much time in hospitals that it was a normal part of life, they were still facing challenges in their daily lives with essential medications or treatment, restrictions in what they were capable of doing and, for these children in particular, social or financial circumstances that added an extra layer of challenge, but the moment they arrived at the castle, those factors became simply a background. A nuisance that wasn't going to interfere with the joy of being here.

The introductory clinic appointments that were part of the settling in process for each child were unlike any clinical consultations Abby had ever performed in a hospital. She was almost literally bowled over by the enthusiastic hug she received from six-year-old Milo and they both made each other laugh. Abby loved the way Milo's whole face crinkled up so much with delight and Milo, well…she'd been right. He took one look at her elf headband and fell in love. He was wearing it himself that afternoon, on top of a woollen hat, when most of the children, bundled up against the cold, went on the expedition to the Scotch pine forest to watch the big tree being felled and choose the small seedlings for their own rooms. The only children who were missing were Callum, who was in a wheelchair and needed supplementary oxygen at all times, and the last-minute additions of Lucy and her brother, Liam, who hadn't arrived yet.

Abby was getting her wish to play with a chainsaw fulfilled. She was being assisted by a group of men from the village, who kept everybody at a safe distance and used ropes to guide the fall of the chosen tree that was at least ten feet tall, and any one of them could have wielded that heavy chainsaw with far more ease than Abby but they made it seem as if they'd never seen it done so well and they led the cheer from everybody watching as the tree toppled. These men had done it many times before and had a flatbed truck ready to take it back to the castle courtyard to be installed and decorated.

The small wilding pines that the children then chose for their rooms only needed a pruning saw to harvest and Milo was one of several children who were keen to try and do it themselves. Abby saw Euan offer a saw to Leah, their heart transplant patient, but the older girl shook her head shyly and clung to her father's hand. Abby left Milo's mum, Louise, to supervise her son with a saw and walked over to join Leah and Euan.

'Would you rather try a chainsaw, sweetheart?'

Leah's jaw dropped and Abby laughed. 'Just kidding. Not that you couldn't use a chainsaw if you wanted to one day but it's a bit safer to start off with a saw like that.'

She pointed to the one Euan was holding, still smiling as she lifted her gaze to his face. They were due to meet later, when the children would be busy making decorations for their trees, to discuss the first appointments and flag any concerns they might have, but they'd been so busy so far that she'd barely seen Euan since they'd come back from their mistletoe gathering this morning. Since that slightly awkward walk back to the castle when neither of them seemed capable of saying anything about what had just happened.

About that kiss...

Little wonder, then, that it was the first thing that crossed Abby's mind as she found those stormy, grey eyes watching her and she knew, she absolutely knew, that it was exactly what Euan was also thinking about. The flicker of sensation deep in her belly exploded into something that was every bit as astonishing as that kiss had turned out to be.

Wow...

Who knew that physical attraction could be *this* potent?

Abby had to look away very quickly. She didn't want Euan, or Leah's father for that matter, getting any hint of what had just flashed through her mind or body. How unprofessional would that be? Euan seemed just as keen to escape. He handed the pruning saw to Abby.

'Why don't you get Abby to show you how it's done?' he suggested to Leah.

Abby could tell that the girl was going to shake her head again so she smiled encouragement. 'How 'bout I start it off for you? That way it'll be easy-peasy.'

'So, did she actually use the saw herself?'

'She did. She needed a bit of hand holding, mind you. She's quite timid, isn't she?'

'Her dad's cautiousness doesn't help. I suspect they've made things harder for each other over the years.'

'He almost dived in and took the saw himself when I held it out.' Abby nodded. 'But I gave him a look.'

Euan's lips twitched. 'Poor man. He didn't stand a chance, did he?'

Abby ducked her head to hide her own smile. This was better. Any awkwardness in the wake of this morning's kiss seemed to have finally evaporated.

'He carried her little tree back for her instead. Leah's busy making coloured paper chains and glittery stars to hang on it now. Did you find anything that we'll need to watch in her physical assessment?'

'She's on quite a few medications, as you'd expect, but her dad's on top of dosages. All her baselines were within normal parameters.'

Abby could feel him watching her, even though she had her gaze on the files she was holding, and it gave her an odd sensation. As if she were dancing—in a floaty, white dress in the middle of a summer forest—instead of sitting here having a professional discussion about young patients.

'I was joking,' Euan said, quietly, a moment later. 'About you intimidating her father. You did well getting her to join in. I'd love to see her with a bit more confidence and enjoy life as much as possible. She's a very lucky girl to have got a transplant. There's far too many who never make it that far.'

Like Fiona? Had she been on a waiting list? Abby looked up but Euan was scanning another set of notes, a frown on his face, even though Leah had been the last child they needed to discuss. She found herself turning her head, to look at the wall in front of Euan's desk in this consulting room. A montage of dozens of photographs plastered the space and they were clearly past participants in Christmas festivities here at the castle.

There were children building snowmen, piled into a big cart that had sides added to make it look like a classic sleigh, ice skating on the lake and receiving gifts from a convincing looking Santa. Such happy photos. And so many different children. Maggie was in many of the images as well and there was one where she was cuddling a small girl with curly, red hair and a smile to rival Milo's in its contagiousness. Just looking at the photograph was enough to make Abby's lips curl. And then look back at Euan.

He looked disconcerted. Because she was smiling at him?

'What?' he demanded.

Abby's smile faded. 'Is that Fiona?' she asked. 'In that photo with Maggie? The little girl with that gorgeous smile?'

'How do you know about Fiona?' But Euan was shaking his head. 'Gammy's been talking to you, hasn't she?'

'She only told me that you had a little sister with HLHS.' *And that he had adored her*... 'She didn't really say anything else. She said it was your story to tell.'

Euan was staring at the wall himself now. He shrugged.

'It's not an unusual story,' he said. 'She had the first surgery—the Norwood procedure—at two weeks old, the Glenn procedure when she was six months and the Fontan just before she turned four.'

During her recent specialist training in paediatric cardiology, Abby had become very familiar with the complex, staged surgeries that could keep a baby alive when the left side of the heart had not developed normally and was unable to provide effective circulation. This clinical information that Euan was sharing was so matter-of-fact and overly concise, it was painfully clear that his very personal experience with the disease was not something he wanted to talk about. Abby simply nodded to let him know that she was listening. She knew there were no cracks in the ice to be felt in these first, tentative steps.

If Euan wanted to change the subject, that was fine. And it seemed that he did.

'There was another child having the same surgeries at about the same time,' he told her. 'Wee Jamie. And he and Fi became the best of friends. They both got out of hospital near Christmas time after the Fontan and Jamie's mother was too exhausted—not to mention couldn't afford—to do anything special to celebrate. Fi saw her crying and wanted to know why. It was her idea to invite them to the castle for Christmas and that was how it all started. The Christmas camp for children just like her.'

'She was a special little girl,' Abby said softly.

'Gammy took the idea and ran with it, of course.' Euan was packing up the folders of medical notes. 'Every year, it got bigger and better with more children being invited and more people from the village becoming involved. Looking back, I think it was important because it gave her something she could control—and make as perfect as possible—when there were so many things that none of us could control that were such a long way from being perfect.'

Abby was sitting very, very still. Euan's

words were calm. Casual, even, but there were undercurrents of emotion here that were huge. So heartbreaking that it wasn't a surprise that Euan was protecting himself by speaking as if it had happened to someone else. The addition of another quiet sentence did come as a surprise, however.

'Fi died when she was seven years old,' Euan said. 'While she was on the waiting list for a transplant.'

So Abby had been right in thinking that his comment about how lucky Leah had been was significant. How devastating must that loss have been for a lad who would have been about fourteen or fifteen and probably coping with not only all the normal teenage stuff but the fact that he'd been the man of the family since his father had died, with three generations of his family that needed protection. Hardly normal teenage things. How strong had he learned to be because of that? Had that been when he'd learned to keep so much buried and locked away?

Abby had to swallow hard. Her heart had already been captured by Euan McKendry's story. Now, she could feel it properly breaking. He hadn't mentioned his mother, either, she realised, and the omission suggested that there was a story all of its own there. It was tempting to ask. To step onto a new patch of ice that might crack beneath her weight. Maybe it was just as well they both heard the quiet tap on the door.

It was Catherine. 'Mrs McKendry sent me to ask if you could both join her in the library if possible,' she told them. 'Those last two weans have arrived finally.'

Lucy Grimshaw was small for her age of five years. She was also one of the most beautiful children Abby had ever seen, with a cascade of bright red curls that reached her shoulders, piercing blue eyes in a pale, pixie face and a smile that reminded Abby of…

Oh, help… It reminded her instantly of that photo of Fiona. So did the hair colour. One glance at Euan's face and she could see the effort it was taking for him to keep his expression so neutral. Judging by the similar effort Maggie was making to hide her own concern, she was very well aware of the extra challenge this was going to present to her grandson. The scowl on Lucy's older brother Liam's face suggested that he was also picking up on the undercurrents. Either that, or he just wasn't happy at all about being here. The lad was sitting very close to his sister and he was quite tall and thin with a darker shade of auburn hair and freckles on his face. The scowl made Abby want to smile, partly because it made her think of what Euan would have been like as a child.

She was acutely aware of Euan behind her right now. He had to need some time to deal with this. Even a few more seconds before he was expected to participate might help.

'Hi, sweetheart.' She went straight to Lucy and crouched down in front of the little girl. 'My name's Abby and this is Dr Euan and we're going to be looking after you while you're here. We're so happy to meet you and your brother. It's Liam, yes?'

Liam wasn't returning even a hint of her smile. He wasn't even going to talk to her, apparently. It was Lucy who nodded in response to the query.

'And I'm Lucy.'

'I know.' Abby's smile widened. 'And do you know why you've come here to the castle?'

'Um… Judith said it was so me and Liam could have Christmas together,' she said.

'A really special Christmas,' Maggie put in. 'And we've got a special room ready for you and Liam to share but I'm guessing you're really hungry and tired after that big car ride.'

'I'm sure they're starving.' The young woman in the room had to be Judith, the social worker, who had brought the children. 'I didn't want to stop anywhere in case it was going to start snowing again and we got stuck. It's all been a bit stressful, to be honest. We got um…held up leaving Edinburgh.'

Catherine had followed Euan and Abby into the library. 'There's lots of nice things in the kitchen for your supper,' she told the children. 'You can choose sausages or fish and chips or spaghetti. And do you like chocolate pudding?'

She held out her hand and Lucy seemed happy to slide off the couch but then she stopped, turned, and held out her small hand to Liam. Clearly, she wasn't brave enough to go somewhere strange without her big brother. The glance between the children as he took her hand brought a big lump to Abby's throat.

'It's okay, Luce,' Liam said, so quietly Abby almost couldn't hear his words. 'I'll look after you.'

Maggie waited until the children had been

taken out of the library to introduce Abby and Euan to Judith.

'Thank you so much for letting us come at the last minute like this,' Judith said. 'It's time out from rather a mess. Lucy and Liam have both been in foster care with the same family since their grandmother died but they just can't cope with the level of care Lucy needs. They said they'd keep Liam but...'

'Oh, no...' Abby didn't dare look at Euan. 'They can't be separated.'

'That's why we got held up leaving. Liam thought I was there to take Lucy to a new home. He locked them both into the bathroom.' Judith was looking as upset as Abby was feeling. 'The only way I could persuade him to open the door was to promise that nothing was going to happen while they were here at the castle but...what happens after Christmas will be out of my hands.'

'Let's not think about that for the moment,' Maggie said calmly. 'Let's just make sure that we give these two beautiful children the best Christmas they could wish for.'

Judith nodded, but her relieved expression vanished as she glanced at the screen of her phone when it began ringing.

'Excuse me... I'll have to take this.' She

rushed towards the door as she answered the call. 'What did the doctor say?' they heard her asking. 'Is he all right?'

She was back a couple of minutes later looking even more stressed than before. 'It's my father,' she told them. 'I knew he was unwell earlier this afternoon and I had to leave it to my mum to take him to the doctor. That was when I was trying to get Liam to unlock that door...' Judith's face was alarmingly pale. 'That was Mum on the phone. She said he had a massive heart attack while he was in the doctor's waiting room and they rushed him to hospital but...but they think he might not make it and...'

'And you need to be there.' Maggie sounded calm and decisive as she got up from her chair and went to put her hand on Judith's arm.

'We can find someone to drive you.' Euan was also moving to offer support. 'I can take you to Inverness and we can arrange transport from there.'

'I can drive,' Judith said. 'It's only a few hours. But... I can't leave the children. And I can't take them to the hospital. And...and I don't know what to do...' She burst into tears.

It was Maggie who took charge. 'Dinna

you worry, pet. You've brought these bairns to exactly the right place. There are any number of people here to give them all the love and care they both need.' It was her grandson's arm she reached out to touch this time. 'Isn't that right, Euan?'

Abby was watching his face as he caught his grandmother's gaze and, again, she was struck by the love between them. She was also caught by the sheer courage she knew it must have taken for Euan to turn and smile so reassuringly at Judith and she felt a squeeze on her heart that felt oddly like pride.

'That's right,' he said. 'We've got this. Now, let's get you sorted with some food and a thermos for the journey and we can tell the children what's happening. Have you got enough petrol? I can arrange for Fergus in the village to open up his garage if it's needed.'

Maggie caught Abby's gaze as Euan and Judith left the room. The shared glance acknowledged what they both knew—that these two new arrivals that they were now to be taking total responsibility for meant that Euan would be facing memories that might be overwhelming.

It was also a shared pact. They were both

going to do whatever they could to make it easier. For everyone, including little Lucy and her big brother who was carrying the weight of the world on his small shoulders.

And, there was something more. It felt as if Abby was somehow tapping into that love she knew existed between Maggie and her grandson. It felt as though Abby was being included in something very precious but, whatever it was, it had the ability to flow in both directions. She could give just as much as she was being given. Or maybe it was just hanging in the air in this remarkable place, as if the love from so many years of this woman's determination to help as many sick children as she could had seeped into the thick, stone walls of this castle.

Like magic.

The kind of magic that Abby had always known Christmas could provide.

CHAPTER FIVE

IT SNOWED AGAIN during the night and it was still snowing as the children and their carers tucked into one of Catherine's legendary breakfasts that was set out as a buffet in the dining room.

'It's a good thing that Christmas cookies are first on our list this morning,' Maggie announced. 'We're going to make and decorate gingerbread men and reindeers and stars and, while that's happening we'll get through our check ups with Dr Abby and Dr Euan. If it stops snowing, we'll be able to have some playtime outside and we can visit the farm animals and make a snowman, perhaps, and later on, we'll be writing our letters to Father Christmas, ready for our sleigh ride tomorrow to post them in the forest.'

She moved to where both Euan and Abby were waiting near the door to collect their first patients for their routine morning visit to the clinic.

'Could you check on Lucy first, please? I put Liam and Lucy into a room close to mine and kept the baby monitor on in case they needed someone in the night.'

'Did they?' Abby asked. She had already turned to look for Lucy amongst the children at one of the long tables. Euan followed her gaze to see Liam wiping what looked like egg yolk off his sister's face with one of the warm, damp cloths a helper was handing out. The way Lucy was laughing and trying to avoid the cloth didn't suggest that she was unwell in any way.

'No.' Maggie shook her head. 'But I think I got woken up a couple of times by Lucy coughing.'

Euan frowned. 'You're not sure?'

'Oh, I know I woke up. I'm just not sure if I actually heard her coughing or if I dreamt it. It had stopped by the time I was properly awake.'

Coughing at night could be an early symptom of heart failure. Something they'd both learned to fear when they heard Fiona coughing at night. Something he'd dreamt about himself, more than once, in the days before he'd learned how to shut things away in that locked space.

'I'll give her a thorough check.'

Abby spoke before Euan had a chance to say anything but he wasn't about to object. It was Abby who had the specialist training, after all, and he could find out what, if anything, there was to be concerned about when they had completed their morning appointments.

But it turned out that Abby wasn't sure either about whether or not there was something to worry about.

'Her baselines are all okay but I'm thinking we might need to adjust her dose of diuretics.'

'Oh? You worried about fluid retention? Increasing heart failure?'

'Her weight hasn't changed since her initial assessment but I could hear some lung sounds that aren't quite what I heard yesterday. Nothing as definite as crackles but her oxygen saturation is already at the lower end of what I'd be looking for. I don't know her well enough to know whether I need to be worried so it's just a gut feeling but I'm planning to watch her carefully.' Abby was smiling now. 'And Liam is obviously planning to watch us carefully. Maggie told me he was watching her like a hawk when she supervised bath time and getting Lucy to bed last night. She even got a lecture about how important it was to be very careful cleaning her teeth so that she doesn't get endocarditis.'

Oh...that released an unexpected memory. He'd known all the vocabulary when he was Liam's age as well.

'But I don't want to clean my teeth. It's boring...'

'You don't want to get bacterial endocarditis, either, so just do it, Fi.'

'You're bossy.'

'I'm your big brother. I'm just looking after you...'

There was a sudden concern to be seen in Abby's eyes. 'You didn't find any problems with the kids who came to you, did you?'

Good grief...how had she picked up so instantly on a flash of memory he'd barely had time to process? Euan was quite confident he wasn't showing anything in his expression but he tightened his mouth into a semblance of a smile, anyway.

'No. It's all good. Milo was sneezing a bit but I think that had more to do with all the flour on his clothing than having picked up a bug. He's an enthusiastic baker, by all accounts.'

It wasn't just the cookie baking that Milo had been enthusiastic about. His decoration involved using icing to glue on as many candy-covered chocolates as possible and he would have eaten them all if his mum hadn't intervened. He was just as excited about getting outside after lunch when it had stopped snowing and he chose Leah to signal, with his hands palm-upwards, making circles in the air.

'That's the sign for "play",' Abby translated. 'Milo wants you to play with him.'

Milo's smile widened until it looked as if it could reach both his ears. 'Pay,' he shouted. 'Pay…' He scooped snow up into his mittened hands and threw it into the air, his laughter such a joyous sound that everyone turned to watch. And Leah was laughing as well. She, too, scooped up snow and threw it up so that it showered down on both of them.

Euan stood to one side. He'd only come out to help with pushing Callum's wheelchair over the uneven brick pathways through the kitchen gardens and had no intention of joining in because they had plenty of helpers, but Abby was making a start on one of the giant snowballs they would need to make the body of a snowman. The new snowfall had obliterated the footprints that he and Abby had made yesterday on their way to the lake but that didn't stop Euan thinking about that walk and he knew what was lying in wait to ambush his brain if he didn't distract himself immediately.

'Are you warm enough, Callum? We can go back inside and watch through the window if you'd rather.'

But Callum shook his head. 'I want to stay.'

'I need some help,' Abby called. 'Milo… stop throwing snow and come and push. This is going to be the biggest snowball in the world.'

'Can I get out of my chair?' Callum begged. 'Can I, Mum? Please? I want to make a snowball too.'

Callum's mother looked at Euan and he had to look away from the shimmer of tears that acknowledged this might be the last time her son would have the opportunity to play in snow.

'I think we can manage that.' Euan carefully lifted the frail child, who was almost hidden under the layers of his warm coat and hat, earmuffs, scarf and mittens, making sure the tubing to the oxygen tank on the back of the wheelchair didn't get disconnected, and helped him shape some snow into a ball that he threw at his mother. The effort was enough to make him short of breath, but he was beaming as Euan put him back into his chair.

'Got you, Mum.'

'You sure did, baby.'

The bottom ball of the snowman was reaching epic proportions by then and several children were helping Abby to keep rolling it.

'Stop,' she called, but the children shrieked with laughter and kept pushing.

'No…*stop*…' The command in Abby's voice this time made everyone freeze and Euan could see that something wasn't right. It was Milo who'd tripped and fallen and now he was lying face down in the snow and wasn't moving. Euan knew what wasn't right, with the same kind of gut feeling that Abby had had about Lucy earlier. This was the unnatural stillness of someone who wasn't conscious.

Someone who possibly wasn't breathing.

He was beside Abby by the time she had turned Milo onto his back and tilted his head to ensure that his airway was open. Louise was only a step or two behind him.

'What's happened?' Louise knelt beside her son. 'Oh, God…is he breathing?'

Abby nodded. 'Yes.' She had her fingers against his neck. 'His heart rate is a little slow but it's picking up. I think he probably fainted.'

Which was a warning that the strenuous activity of rolling the huge snowball could have been too much for his heart to cope with.

'Let's get him into the clinic so we can check him out properly.' Euan crouched to pick Milo up and found that the little boy was waking up. For once, he wasn't smiling.

'Mum?'

'I'm here, darling. It's okay…'

Euan was bracing himself to pick Milo up from the ground without injuring his back but Milo made it much easier by reaching up to wrap his arms around Euan's neck and trying to get to his feet himself. By the time Euan was upright, Milo was clinging to him like a solid little monkey, hanging on tight with both his arms and legs. He felt increasingly heavy by the time Euan got to the clinic, having left the volunteer helpers and carers in charge of the snowman building, but it wasn't simply the weight that was becoming progressively harder to cope with—it was this intensely close physical contact with a child and he felt as if his heart were being squeezed even more tightly than his body. At least he could be thankful that it hadn't been Lucy who'd collapsed. She might be as light as a feather but Euan didn't even want to think about how it would have felt to carry her in his arms.

It was a huge relief to put Milo down on the bed in the consulting room and let Abby step in to start the assessment.

'Shall we get Mum to come and sit on the bed with you?' Abby suggested.

Milo nodded and cuddled up to Louise while Abby listened to his chest with her stethoscope.

'How long ago did Milo have the balloon dilation of the aortic valve?'

'Over a year, now. They did say that it might need to be done again but...but that if it wasn't enough, he might need another operation.'

'And this is the first time he's fainted?'

'Yes. He did have that episode where he

got very short of breath not so long ago, though.'

Abby nodded, focused on what she was hearing and trying to make the rest of her assessment no big deal for Milo.

'I'm going to put these sticky dots on your chest, now, sweetheart. And this little crocodile on your finger.' She opened and shut the pulse oximeter clip a few times. 'It doesn't hurt,' she promised. 'See?'

She put the clip on her nose and Milo laughed out loud, circling his hands in the sign for 'play'. He laughed again when she put the clip on his own nose briefly before shifting it to a fingertip and Euan heard his own chuckle escape. He also felt the weight he hadn't realised he was still carrying lift from his heart. By the time he and Abby were having a quiet lunch in the castle kitchen, to avoid the noise and busyness of the dining rooms, he could talk about what had happened with his normal and totally appropriate professionalism.

'I don't think it's an emergency by any means,' he said in response to Abby's query. 'I agree that it was a result of all that effort he was putting into pushing the snowball and, if he avoids that kind of strenuous activity, it's not likely to happen again. And it's not as if they're going to do any major investigations right before Christmas, like an exercise stress test or a catheterisation to get accurate pressure measurements above and below the aortic valve.'

'It's best that he goes back to the team who've been looking after him since birth for any of that.' Abby nodded.

'But I would quite like to get an echo done, just for peace of mind.'

Again, Abby nodded. 'Louise is putting a brave face on things but it's obvious that this has given her a huge fright. And made her realise that more open-heart surgery could well be on the cards. Milo could be picking up on that. He was quite subdued after his ECG. Even the elf headband didn't cheer him up.'

Abby looked as if she needed a bit of cheering up herself. She was using her spoon to stir the delicious vegetable soup Cath had provided for their lunch but seemed to have lost her appetite. Perhaps they all needed some reassurance so they could relax and enjoy the next few days.

'How 'bout I ring my friend in Inverness and see if they've got time to see Milo for an echo this afternoon?'

'Oh…that would be wonderful. Do you think they'll be able to see him?'

'I'm sure they will. We might have to wait a while but they all go out of their way to help any of our camp kids. I'll drive them in and we might even be back in time for dinner.' It was good to hear Abby's sigh of relief but what Euan really wanted was to see her smile again.

'I'll leave you to keep watch on everybody else for the afternoon. Are you going to write a letter to Father Christmas? And decorate the envelope, of course—that's obligatory. That way, you'll get to post it in the elves' post box tomorrow.' He lowered his voice to a secretive whisper. 'It's actually a big, old hollow tree in the oak forest that we cut a slot into. There's twenty years' worth of kids' letters inside that trunk.'

'What?' Abby was feigning horror. 'You mean the letters don't get to the North Pole?'

Euan's lips twitched. 'The sleigh ride is a camp highlight for the kids and we get some of the best photographs from it. Just wait till you see Bonnie and Scotch with their antlers on and bells all over their harnesses. It's quite a sight.'

The degree of pleasure that he had succeeded in making Abby smile was like an upward swoop on the emotional rollercoaster Euan seemed to be riding today.

'I can't wait. And, you know what?'

'What?'

'I think I will write that letter. There's something I'd love this Christmas.'

'What's that?'

'Can't say. If I tell, it might not happen. Christmas secrets, you know?'

'Mmm…'

But the way Abby was looking at him made Euan wonder if what she was wishing had something to do with him. Or maybe the wish was *for* him, which wouldn't be a surprise at all because he was beginning to realise how big a heart this woman had. How much love she had to give others. Maybe that was why she loved Christmas so much? Because it was a time to not hold back in showering the people around her with love? A bit of that squeeze had come back to enclose Euan's heart. That man who would father her six children currently had no idea how lucky he was, did he?

It was well after dinner time when Euan got back to the castle that evening. The usual buzz of getting all the children fed, bathed and into bed was well and truly over.

'How are you?' Maggie came out of the kitchen holding a couple of hot water bottles in bright woollen covers. 'How's Milo?'

'It's all good,' Euan assured her. 'We'll stop him doing anything too strenuous and there shouldn't be any more problems for now.'

'Oh, thank goodness. I was so worried.' Maggie didn't have to stoop far to give Milo a kiss. 'Are you hungry? Cath has got something in the oven for you all if you are.'

'We ate in the hospital cafeteria while we were waiting for the echo,' Louise told her. 'I expect Milo would like another one of his Christmas cookies but I'd better get this tired wee boy into bed and I might say goodnight as well. We've had a big day.' She reached into her shoulder bag. 'Something else we did while we were waiting…' She pulled out a large envelope. 'Someone was kind enough to make up a pack so Milo wouldn't miss out on the letter writing. I think posting the letter into that tree is his favourite part of camp.'

'Oh, lovely. Euan, can you take that, please? I've got to take these hotties up to Lucy and

Liam. The box is in the drawing room. We'll do the list later, after everyone's gone to bed.'

In the end, however, Euan made sure that Maggie had taken some more painkillers and ordered her off to bed to rest and wouldn't listen to any objections. 'If you're not looking any better in the morning, it'll be you I'll be taking in to the hospital,' he warned her.

Maggie sighed. 'He's only saying that because he knows the sleigh ride is my favourite thing. All right... I'll go and get some sleep.' She put the box on the sofa between Euan and Abby and handed a folder to her grandson. 'You know what to do.'

He did. But Abby's jaw dropped when she saw him carefully open the first letter he took from the box.

'What are you *doing*?'

'Reading the letters. Oh, aye, I know about the Christmas secrets, but this is what we do.'

'Why?'

'So that we can try to make sure the children get something they've asked for.' Euan picked up the folder. 'The parents bring one gift, which is hidden away to go under the tree on Christmas Eve. We've got a list of what they are, so we don't double up on anything. Each child has a stocking that goes on their door handle and that's full of little treats that get donated. We also get funding from various charities and we use some of that to provide a gift that Santa gives them from his sack. That's Fergus, by the way, from the garage in the village. He makes a good Father Christmas, does Fergus.'

He unfolded the first letter. 'This is from Leah,' he told her. 'And what she wants most of all is a puppy. That's a no-no.'

'Because she's not allowed a puppy?'

'Because puppies are for ever and not just for Christmas,' Euan said. 'Besides, imagine the chaos on Christmas Day if we had puppies running around the castle?'

But Abby didn't smile back. 'So what will Leah get from Father Christmas, then?'

'A toy puppy.' Euan was making a note on a blank sheet of paper. 'And we'll have a word with her dad. If it's a possibility, he can tell her that there might be a real puppy down the track. Caring for a pet may be a good way for Leah to gain a bit of confidence.'

'Hmm.' Abby seemed distracted. She was peering into the box. 'You're not opening my letter,' she told him. 'And that's that.'

'Fair enough. The last time I put a letter in that box I knew I had to keep it a secret.'

'I'll look after this one.' Abby wasn't looking at him as she pulled an envelope from the box and put it to one side. 'Did you get *your* wish?'

Euan pretended he was also busy, reading the next letter, so he could ignore the query. 'Louise has written this for Milo and he's done the decorating. He wants a computer game, which will be easy. She'll give us his device and we can load the app.'

When some requests were already being provided, the shopping list got a question mark so that parents could be consulted about a surprise. There were no more requests for puppies and most were doable. Until the last.

'Oh…' It was Abby who was reading the letter. 'This is a joint request. From Lucy and Liam.' She looked up at Euan and he was shocked to see the tears filling her eyes. 'They just want to be able to stay together…' Her voice broke and a tear trickled down the side of her nose. 'Because…because they love each other.'

Euan found himself on his feet without conscious movement. He wanted to turn and head for the door and escape but…he couldn't go any further. He couldn't walk away from Abby when she was looking like this. When she needed comfort. Slowly, he sat back down again, shifting the box so that it wasn't between them.

'It's never easy, is it?' he said quietly. 'Being with these kids.'

Abby swiped the tear off her cheek. 'We can't make this one come true, can we?'

'No. But Maggie will have an idea of something special we can do for them. Maybe we can take a heap of photos and make books for them. Memories…'

'That's a lovely idea.' Abby sniffed, clearly trying to stem her tears. She was even trying to smile at him and Euan could feel a very odd squeeze in his chest at the way her voice wobbled when she spoke again.

'When was it?' she asked. 'That you wrote your last letter to Father Christmas? And what was it that you kept secret?'

Oh, damn…those tears were contagious, judging by the way his throat was constricting. And, while that part of his body was tightening up, another part felt as if it were cracking open.

'I was fourteen,' he said. 'And I asked for the same thing that Fi had asked for in *her* letter.' He had to stop and swallow hard. 'I suspect Maggie still has that letter some-where.' Not that he'd seen it in more than twenty years, but it was still there in his mind as clearly as when he'd first opened that en-velope. That picture of an angel and the care-ful letters of a seven-year-old.

Dear Father Christmas
Please can I have a new heart?
That's all.
Thank you very much.
Love from Fi

'She only asked for one thing,' Euan whis-pered aloud. 'A new heart...'

To his horror, he could feel a tear roll-ing down his own face. Even more disturb-ing was the way that Abby threw her arms around him. No...what was doing his head in completely was how much he'd wanted her to do exactly that. To rediscover the kind of human comfort that he'd never sought as an adult. To offer that comfort as well, to some-one else who was feeling sad.

He had no idea how long they simply sat and held each other but the fire had died down to glowing coals by the time he raised his head. Abby shifted as well and there they were, again, as they had been under the apple tree, so close that it would take no effort at all to kiss her. Even the thought of doing that made it irresistible. Euan wasn't even sure if he made the first move because it just seemed to happen and…dear Lord…it was even more unbelievable than the first time. That softness. The taste. The warmth that was so much more than purely physical. It was wrapping itself around his heart but stirring other parts of his body in a way he'd never experienced.

He'd never wanted to be with anyone this much. To be as close as it was physically possible to be.

It was Abby who said it, though, as they finally ended that kiss.

'Let's go to bed,' she said softly.

And, there it was.

The life-saver.

The most enticing way to step away from reality for just a little while. And, okay, he knew there was too much emotion involved, here. That, normally, he'd back off as far and fast as possible until he'd got his own head together. But…

But there had been too many downward

swoops in today's rollercoaster. That reminder of how hearing coughing during the night could spark fear and how important a simple task like cleaning teeth could become. That look in Callum's mother's eyes as she got a glimpse into what they both knew the future held. That overwhelming experience of carrying Milo in his arms.

And now this. The comfort being offered in the wake of the hardest memory of all. That single request that Fi had made with total trust that the magic of Christmas could make it happen.

He'd wanted to believe, as well. He'd desperately needed that hope.

As much as he needed the comfort he knew that Abby could give him now. The comfort he knew he could give *her*.

As he got to his feet, he let his hand slide down Abby's arm until it caught her hand and, as he felt her fingers tighten around his, Euan knew without a shadow of a doubt that she wanted this intimate time together as much as he did.

There was definitely magic here, within the walls of this castle.

There was the glow of firelight and the

twinkle of Christmas lights on the tree. The suits of armour in the entrance foyer were sporting red hats with white trim and pom poms and there were ropes of ivy and more sparkling lights wound through the stair bannisters and the balustrade above. There was even a wreath that Maggie had somehow found time to make from the mistletoe they'd gathered yesterday hanging beneath the enormous chandelier just in front of staircase.

Was that why Euan paused just there? Why he wove his fingers through Abby's hair to cup the back of her neck, holding her still while he kissed her again, with a thoroughness that drove any other thoughts from her mind—including how unprofessional it would seem if anyone saw them.

No one had ever kissed her like this. She'd never wanted to be with anyone like this. Was that because Euan McKendry was so completely the opposite of any man she would have considered to be her 'type'? That didn't matter a jot right now. This was about how she'd caught more than simply an echo of the kind of loss Euan had to be feeling. That scare of seeing Milo so motionless on the ground today. The sadness of knowing that Lucy, a child she had already fallen in love with, could be facing not only a limited future but that she might have to do it without the big brother she adored. To see Euan shed tears had been a point of no return, however. She could see through that grumpy façade so easily now. She could see the boy who'd been hurt so much he'd had to wall himself off to survive. The man who was still capable of that kind of love but too afraid to let it into his life. She could feel the whole weight of what he was facing for the next few days. Abby could also feel the ice of those barriers he'd built starting to crack all around her feet as she held his hand and climbed the stairs with him to her bedroom.

They walked silently along the hallway, past the closed doors that were offering them a safe passage to the room where the door could be clicked shut on something that could be kept completely private. Abby closed her eyes as she leaned on that door, her arms around Euan's neck as she stood on tiptoes to kiss him again.

He started to say something but she put her finger against his lips, smiling into his eyes as she tried to tell him, silently, that nothing needed to be said. That neither of them needed to overthink this in any way. This was a moment in time in which Euan could completely escape. That Abby was more than happy to go with him. She saw the moment when he took that first step into the delicious oblivion she knew they were going to find. When his eyes darkened and slowly closed as his lips covered hers, his hands sliding down her back to bring her hips in contact with the hardness of his body.

The tiny sound of need escaping Abby's lips got swallowed by Euan but he must have heard it because he moved his hand to stroke her skin beneath her clothes and then grasped the hem of her jumper to pull it up and over her head. And then his fingers were deftly undoing the buttons of her shirt and a sense of urgency became so strong that Abby had to let her own hands find Euan's bare skin and she, too, let everything else go to be completely in the moment. Being totally naked and cocooned in the feathery softness of that wonderful bed that was temporarily her own couldn't happen soon enough.

Never mind what she'd written in her private letter to Father Christmas. This was going to be her gift to Euan this Christmas—

the joy of human connection and comfort. Of desire and release.

And, tonight, maybe she needed it herself, just as much.

CHAPTER SIX

THIS HAD TO be up there with the best moments ever in Abby Hawkins' life.

To be snuggled up in faux fur rugs, with a small person to cuddle on her lap, and two of the biggest and most beautiful horses she had ever seen, with bells jingling all over their harnesses and clouds of steam puffing from their nostrils as they slowly pulled the enormous cartload of adults and children along a wide track through the oak forest and towards the lake.

Abby hadn't stopped smiling from the moment she'd joined the children in the farmyard as the final preparations were being made to the horses and sleigh. The castle's cow, Daisy, and the very friendly mob of pet sheep were watching the excitement through a fence and the donkeys, Joseph and Mary, had their heads over the half-door in their stable.

Euan had been helping to make sure the antlers were firmly secured to the horses' bridles when Abby had arrived and she hadn't been able to resist the pull to go to his side.

'They look so real,' Abby said. 'And super heavy?'

'They are real deer antlers.' Euan's face might be as serious as always, but there was a smile in his eyes as he spoke to her. 'They've been cleverly carved to make them lighter. It was Fergus's father that made them—more than twenty years ago now—when he was in his nineties, no less.'

Having made sure that Lucy was well wrapped up in her hat and scarf, Maggie joined them to reach up and stroke the nose of the horse that was towering above her. The way she didn't move when the horse snorted loudly and bobbed its head had made Abby smile even more. She was getting very fond of this feisty, small woman whom she could only hope would also be doing something remarkable in her nineties.

'Climb up,' Euan had instructed Abby. 'You can be Lucy's carer this morning. Maggie's going to sit up front and take the reins, as usual. I'll be walking, with Leah's dad.' He'd lowered his voice so that only Abby could hear. 'We're going to have a wee chat about puppies.'

So here she was, with Lucy on her lap and Liam sitting beside her in the back corner of an old hay cart that had been customised to look like a silver and white sleigh with runners that were low enough to almost hide the wheels behind them.

'Isn't this exciting? Are you warm enough, sweetheart?'

Lucy nodded. Like Abby, she couldn't stop smiling. She poked her brother. 'Have you still got our letter, Liam? I'm the one who's going to post it, aren't I?'

'Yep.' But Liam didn't even glance at the carefully resealed letter he had in his hands. He was staring through the trees beside him and then he pointed at something. 'What's over there?'

'It's a lake.'

'The one we get to go ice-skating on?'

'Yes. If it's safe enough. Dr Euan hasn't checked it yet. I think the skating is something we do on Christmas Day.' She gave Lucy another cuddle. 'How many sleeps is it now?'

'Two.'

'That's right. Two sleeps. Just as well we're getting our letters posted today, isn't it? I think Father Christmas is going to be very busy trying to get organised.'

This time, Liam did turn his head and the look he gave Abby finally dimmed her smile. Had it sounded as if she might be making an excuse for the non-delivery of their request? He couldn't know that she knew what he'd asked for in the letter he was holding but she felt as if he was blaming her for something. For being yet another adult that couldn't be trusted, perhaps? For perpetuating a myth that there was a Father Christmas who could grant wishes? Liam looked as if he knew perfectly well that any promises she might offer would be broken.

Was he already growing up to hate Christmas as much as Euan?

The boy didn't hold Abby's gaze long enough for her to try and offer any kind of reassurance, which was probably just as well because the only thing she could do was send a silent plea out into the universe that a miracle might happen and that these children could stay together for as long as possible.

Of course Abby knew that there was no

Father Christmas in the North Pole but she did believe in miracles. In magic. A kind of magic that had nothing to do with fairies and wands, or wizards and spells, mind you. The kind of magic she had every faith in was about people caring and the amazing alchemy that could result in unexpected and beautiful things happening.

Abby let her gaze drift over the heads of the other children in the cart. Callum's wheelchair had been left behind and he, like Lucy, was wrapped in an incredibly soft rug, safe in his mother's arms. Milo was cuddled up beside Louise, laughing aloud with every jolt of the cart as it encountered tree roots on its path. There was Maggie on the front bench, with Leah sitting beside her, and Leah was helping to hold the reins, as Maggie called encouragement to the horses. Bonnie and Scotch were plodding steadily on and Euan McKendry was one of the people walking by their shoulders. For a long, delicious moment, Abby let her gaze rest on him.

She'd experienced some of the kind of that magic she believed in herself, only last night.

The trust Euan had offered her by making himself so vulnerable—coming apart in her arms, even—wasn't the most extraordinary aspect of the best sex she'd ever had, though. It was that this man, who'd so badly needed an escape from reality and ghosts from the past, could still care about her and that her needs were being met. To be such a generous lover. To be that gentle and sensitive and yet so astonishingly masculine at the same time. To control that strength in the height of passion and be so aware of his partner was the sexiest thing ever.

Her breath came out in a sigh that made Lucy look up, so Abby smiled down at the little pixie face that was so heartbreakingly gorgeous.

'Two sleeps,' she whispered. She didn't look at Liam again. Two days and two sleeps were a blip in time but maybe something good would happen. It wasn't beyond the realms of possibility that someone with a heart as big as Louise's might be found and be willing to open their home and heart to these two children.

Two sleeps until Christmas.

Three sleeps until Abby was due to leave Ravenswood Castle.

She found herself watching Euan again. Would he need—or want—any more time out? Another…escape? *She* wanted it, that was for sure. If anything, the level of attraction she was feeling was snowballing, rather like that enormous stomach of the snowman she'd been in charge of creating before that scary incident with Milo yesterday. Given that it was already at a higher level than she'd ever felt in her life before, at least Abby could be confident that this physical desire wasn't going to become any more of a distraction. And that she could control it, when she needed to.

'There it is,' someone called. 'There's the tree.'

And there it was. A tall trunk that was the remains of a forest giant that had toppled long ago, with a slot cut into it at a level that a small person could reach if they stood on tiptoes. Around the base of the tree trunk was a collection of carvings. Big mushrooms with doors in their stalks and tiny elves in their gardens or workshops. It was a work of art that was enchanting. Surely even Liam couldn't be entirely certain that there wasn't a bit of magic involved in posting their special letters?

He did seem to be as captured as everybody else, including Abby. It was Liam who led Lucy by the hand to see the elven village up close and he was the one to lift his little sister so that she could post the letter. There was a professional photographer amongst the entourage on foot, snapping images of the occasion, but Abby had her phone out as well and the image she caught of Lucy's face as she slid that envelope through the slot was one she knew she would keep for the rest of her life. It wasn't just the glow of complete faith from Lucy that her Christmas wish was going to the one place and person who could make it come true, it was the expression of pure love on her brother's face as he watched her. The combination added up to something even bigger.

It felt like hope.

Abby was blinking back tears as she looked up from her screen to find Euan watching her and, for a heartbeat, that eye contact felt as intimate as anything physical that had happened between them last night. A wash of something astonishingly soft and warm rippled through Abby's body and, weirdly, that felt like hope as well, along with the certainty that their time together hadn't been a one-off. That they both wanted it to happen again.

* * *

The Christmas Camp programme was ramping up, which added pressure to finding the time to monitor all the children closely and deal with any medical issues without unduly disrupting their participation in activities.

On a personal level, Euan always found that he had to distance himself more and more from things that weren't medical as the anticipation built and there were specific activities he usually avoided like the plague. The Christmas themed dress up party at the castle tonight was one of those activities. So was the posting of letters in the elf tree. He'd gone along today, however, and while he'd told himself it was because he was keeping an extra eye on Milo and because he wanted to make sure Maggie wasn't doing anything that would make her pain level harder to manage, Euan knew that wasn't the whole story.

He'd gone on the sleigh ride because Abby had gone. Because he wanted to be close enough to be able to see her and talk to her. Because moments between and after the morning health checks hadn't been enough. Most of all, it was because he felt safe. It would only take a glance and he'd be able to tap into a distraction that could override any ghosts that were lying in wait for him. It would be no effort at all to remember what last night had been like. It would, in fact, be a pleasure to give in to the temptation to re-live every touch. Every kiss. Every delicious stolen moment of being completely oblivi-ous to the outside world. He'd been right in thinking that his attraction to Abby could be a life-saver and that had been when he'd only experienced what it was like to kiss her. Now he knew what it was like to fall into an exquisite, physical oblivion in her company and that had increased any distracting power exponentially.

To his astonishment, he had genuinely en-joyed the sleigh ride this morning.

And he was quite agreeable to Maggie's request that he got his bagpipes out for the period of time the children were warming up in the drawing room before lunch so that they could have a quick choir practice.

'As you will have seen on our programme, we go down to the village church for the carol service on Christmas Eve,' Maggie told everybody who'd gathered to soak in the warmth of the fire after their chilly outing to the forest. 'Euan pipes us in and we're carrying our candles and then the bagpipes fade away when we're at the front of the church and we start singing and then everybody else joins in.'

'Oh, that sounds lovely.' It was Ben's grandmother who spoke up. 'What carol will it be? We've been practising at home from the list ever since we knew we were coming to camp.'

'"The Little Drummer Boy". One of my absolute favourites.' Maggie beamed at everyone. 'Euan's going to play a little bit for you now, just so you know how loud it is. We don't want anyone getting a fright tomorrow night. Are you ready, Euan?'

'Aye.'

Euan already had already taken his set of bagpipes out of their wooden case. He had the bag under his arm and the drones on his shoulder. He lifted the blowpipe to his mouth.

'You can put your fingers in your ears if you need to,' Maggie called as he blew his first breath into the bag and the background base of the drones started to sound.

Even though he was on the far side of the enormous room, it was piercingly loud to be doing this inside and, as Euan increased the air in the bag to provide enough pressure to add the chanter notes of the song to the background, he saw Lucy, who was sitting on Abby's lap again, clap her hands over her ears. She looked as if she might be gleefully shrieking as well but he couldn't hear that over the sound of the Christmas song. Abby, along with many of the carers, were looking impressed but slightly overwhelmed. Liam's jaw had dropped and he was simply staring, mesmerised. And he wasn't covering his ears to try and muffle the sound.

Playing the bagpipes had been another kind of life-saver for Euan all those years ago, when he'd been dealing with unimaginable loss, but he only used this instrument when he was at the castle these days and that wasn't nearly often enough. It was fortunate that he could play this song, and many other Christmas carols, from memory. It only took one verse and a chorus to knock any rust off his skills and that was enough to be doing inside for now. Maggie and her helpers, including Muriel with her small, portable keyboard, were ready to fill the silence by leading the singing from the children. Euan watched for a moment as he silenced the pipes.

Maggie was looking pale, he thought. And

tired. Whether she liked it or not, he was going to take her over to the clinic and check her blood pressure and other vital signs and find out exactly how much pain she was in and any other symptoms she could well be hiding. He found himself sighing as he laid the pipes back in their case. What was going to happen when Maggie was no longer here? Would he even come to the castle at all? Would these wonderful old pipes that his father and his grandfather before him had played stay in their case and never be heard? His grandmother had never pushed past his reluctance to discuss his inheritance but the fact that this could be the last Christmas camp ever at Ravenswood Castle was another level of pressure that was ramping up.

Time could well be running out.

The savoury smell of the hot pasties Cath was serving for lunch was all the more inviting after the fresh air and excitement of the morning's expedition.

'Cornish pasties. Yum.' Abby lifted Lucy onto her chair and left another clear for Liam.

'Och, no.' Cath shook her head. 'These are Forfar bridies, lass. There's no potatoes in these so they're much tastier. There's home-made tomato sauce there, too, if you like it.'

Abby liked it very much. So did Lucy. What was threatening to spoil her enjoyment, however, was that Liam's chair beside her was still empty.

'He's taking a long time to wash his hands. Will you be all right for a minute while I go and find him, Lucy?'

Lucy nodded around a mouthful of bridie, a big smear of sauce on her chin, but Abby still paused as she left the dining room to let Maggie know she'd left the little girl to eat the rest of her lunch alone.

There was no sign of Liam in the foyer. Euan was there, however, and he looked far from happy.

'What's happened?'

'My bagpipes have vanished.'

'What? Where were they?'

'Right there, in their case.' Euan pointed at the empty wooden box on an ornately carved sideboard near the doors to the drawing room. 'I had something I wanted to do in the clinic and I've just come back. Who would have taken them? And why? One of the children, do you think? To play with them?'

Abby shook her head. 'They went to wash

their hands straight after the singing practice. And then we all went to the dining room. Everyone was starving by then.'

Euan had to be hungry himself and Abby had the strongest urge to see him tucking into one of Cath's wonderful bridies but she could see that he was upset. There were tight lines around his eyes and dark shadow within them.

'They were my father's,' he told her. 'And my grandfather's before that. They're not a toy.'

No. They were something very precious but she'd already known that, hadn't she? The way the hairs on the back of her neck had prickled when she'd heard the first notes of the bagpipes had told her that and Euan's body language as he'd stood there playing had been...well...that had also touched something very deep in Abby.

'Oh...' She pressed her fingers to her mouth. 'Liam hasn't come in to lunch. That's why I've come out. To find him.'

It wasn't hard to put two and two together.

'Where would he go?' Euan's scowl was ferocious now. 'And what's he doing with the pipes? I thought he *liked* hearing them.

He was one of the only bairns who didn't put their fingers in their ears.'

'There must be a million places to hide inside this castle,' Abby said. 'Let alone outside it.' She bit her lip. 'He wouldn't go far away from Lucy, though. Maybe he's gone to the only place he's ever alone with her?'

'His room?'

Euan was already heading for the sweep of the staircase, his face tightening with what looked like anger. Abby raced after him, hoping desperately that they weren't going to find those heirloom bagpipes damaged in any way. She'd seen Euan annoyed. She'd seen him walk away from things that he didn't like, but she'd never seen him lose control due to anger. Liam might need protection. *Euan* might need it himself.

She was moving so quickly as she went through the door of the children's bedroom that she bumped into Euan's back because he'd stopped as soon as he'd entered the room. He was standing very still, staring at the enormous bed that Liam and Lucy were sharing. Liam was sitting in the middle of the bed. He was clearly trying to hold the bagpipes the way he'd seen Euan holding them earlier and he had the pipe for blowing in his mouth but the ungainly instrument looked far too big and it had a life of its own, with the pipes rolling off Liam's shoulder as Abby watched.

Liam was staring back at Euan and he looked terrified—as if he knew that he was about to be severely punished. Abby wanted nothing more than to go to his side. To put her arm around him and offer support but she knew this was between Liam and Euan. She knew that Liam would have to face up to being told he'd done something he shouldn't have. She could only hope that Euan wouldn't be too hard on him. What Euan actually did, however, took her breath away.

He went and sat on the edge of the bed. He was looking at his hands, rather than directly at Liam, when he spoke.

'So…you fancy learning to play the pipes, do you, lad?'

Liam said nothing. He was hanging his head, staring down at the bagpipes he'd taken, and Abby had never seen him look more miserable.

'It's not an easy thing to learn. I started when I was about your age…and it was something I wanted to do because I missed my daddy and these were *his* pipes so they were very special to me.'

Oh… That lump in Abby's throat was enough to block her breathing. Like the way she had been able to time travel and see a happy young boy climbing that apple tree beside the lake, she could see a slightly older and very different boy now. One that was aching for his daddy and trying, too soon, to fill his shoes. A courageous boy, now a man, who had a direct connection to another boy who was struggling with what life was presenting. And that raw emotion in his quiet words was touching a deep part of her soul. This was the real Euan, wasn't it? The one that was normally kept so well hidden.

This was a man who protected himself by growling at the world to keep people at bay but he was offering a door in those barriers to this boy. And this was a boy who was so unhappy that he was unwilling to trust or respond to anyone. Except that he was slowly turning his head now, so that he could look up at the man sitting on the end of the bed.

'The thing is, you don't learn by what you're doing now. That's like jumping into the middle of a lake before you've learned to swim a bit closer to the shore. When you start to learn the pipes, you play what's called a practice chanter. Same as this bit on the pipes...' Euan touched a part of the instrument '...but it's smaller and easier—like a recorder. I could show you mine if you like?'

Abby's heart was melting and, as she saw Liam's slow, shy nod, she found herself edging backwards so that she could leave this man and boy together. She needed a moment to herself, anyway, because it was in that moment that she realised there was far more than simply an irresistible physical attraction between herself and Euan McKendry. He might be the total opposite of someone she could see in her future but that hadn't stopped it happening, had it?

She was falling in love with him. So fast and so hard there was no chance of stopping it happening and it already felt as if her heart were about to break into a million pieces because it was too full. And, maybe, because it was the first time she'd felt *this* strongly about anyone and it was only going to last— *could* only last—until she left Ravenswood Castle, which meant there could be heartbreak ahead.

Only three sleeps away.

CHAPTER SEVEN

'YOU DISAPPEARED.'

He'd noticed? Even when he had been so clearly focused on dealing with a rather significant development in Liam's visit to the castle? Abby was aware of a frisson of something that felt curiously like…hope? She kept her tone carefully casual, though.

'I could see that Liam was ready to have a serious man-to-man talk about bagpipes. And I could see that you had it all in hand.'

Euan's glance acknowledged her unspoken approval for the way he had handled the incident of the borrowed bagpipes. Then he frowned. 'Your cheeks are very pink.'

He touched one very gently with the back of his fingers. 'And very cold.'

They must be almost frozen, Abby thought, because the heat coming from that light touch was so hot it was scorching. Euan blinked, as if he'd felt it as well.

'Have you been outside?'

'I went out to the stables.' Abby found a bright smile, confident she wouldn't reveal any of the emotional overload that had sent her off to find a quiet spot to get her head together. But, just in case, she offered an excuse for anything that might slip past her guard. 'I think I'm in love with Joseph and Mary. There's something about donkeys, isn't there?'

'Hmph…' Euan's grunt—and the way he looked away from her—suggested that he was back within his own defensive walls. 'They might deserve their place in a nativity scene, which is what Christmas is really about rather than the commercial circus we've since created, but I think Maggie went a wee bit overboard in naming them.'

A commercial circus? Oh, yeah… Euan was definitely well over that deeply personal moment he'd had with Liam.

'It's more than that. They're such gentle creatures. Serene, even. Just standing beside them can make you feel kind of peaceful.'

Thankfully, they'd made Abby feel a lot more in control, anyway. Okay, maybe she *was* falling in love with Euan but it didn't have to be a disaster at all. She could actually embrace it, knowing that it was only going to last a few days and then she could tuck it away. In the same place that she'd filed youthful crushes on movie stars or pop idols, perhaps, where nothing could ever come of it but it was rather delicious to play with. Mind you, she'd never gone to bed with any movie star or pop idol, had she?

'Ah…there you are, Euan.' Maggie was walking towards them. Slowly. A little unevenly, as if she was leaning to one side.

'Are you limping, Gammy?'

She shrugged. 'Maybe a little. Did you finally get some lunch? And what about Liam?'

'Don't change the subject. Are you hurting? I thought you were looking poorly earlier. Come over to the clinic with me so I can have a look at you.'

Maggie shook her head firmly. 'I've got far too much to do. We're just getting the children all settled for quiet time with a movie and stories so they won't be too tired for the party this evening.'

'You need quiet time too. There's plenty of helpers here. They can do whatever needs to be done and you know you only need to ask. Where are you off to now?'

'I'm on my way up to the attics on the south side, in the servants' quarters over the kitchens, and, I must admit, I wasn't looking forward to all those steep stairs.' There was a gleam in Maggie's eyes that made Abby want to smile. Even at this age and unwell, she was a woman who knew how to get what she wanted.

'What on earth do you need to go up there for?'

'The dress ups. We got the boxes of decorations down a couple of weeks ago but the party costumes got forgotten.'

'You shouldn't be climbing unnecessary stairs, let alone lugging heavy boxes.' Euan glanced over his shoulder as if he was hoping a helpful volunteer would be wandering around but the only other person here was Abby and his outward breath sounded exasperated. 'I'll get them,' he said. 'But only if you go and put your feet up for a while, Gammy. And take your pills. If you're still sore when I come back, you're coming over to the clinic with me and no arguments. Or I'll call Graham and drag him out from the village to give you a piece of his mind about not taking good enough care of yourself.'

Maggie's outward breath was a rather satisfied one. She ignored the warning and smiled at Abby instead.

'Euan could take you with him up to the attics,' she said. 'He'll need some help with all those boxes. I know there are parts of the castle we keep closed off because it's just too big to look after it all, but you'd like to see a bit more of the parts that are open, wouldn't you, pet?'

'I really would.' Abby nodded. She smiled at Euan. 'Can we go now?'

They had to go past the kitchens to get to the back stairs that led to the old servants' quarters and the attic above them and the enticing, savoury smell floating into the hall was irresistible.

'I do believe I can smell bacon. And I'm starving. I didn't get any lunch.' Euan veered into the kitchen. 'Catherine, you wouldn't be cooking some pigs in blankets, now, would you?'

The cook laughed. 'They've been your favourite since you were a wee laddie. Here…' She pointed to a tray on top of one of the ovens. 'You can have a taste. We're just start-ing to do the cooking for tonight's party.'

As always, the tiny chipolata sausage wrapped in crispy bacon made the most de-licious mouthful ever. Euan picked another up by its toothpick to offer it to Abby and, without thinking, he held it up to her mouth and then watched closely as she delicately took the sausage off the toothpick with her teeth and lips, closing her eyes almost in-stantly in the sheer pleasure of the taste.

His own pleasure of seeing Abby enjoying something he was so fond of himself gave Euan an odd feeling—as if it was something he could be proud of, which was ridiculous. And that it was something he wanted to do again. And again. Which was disconcert-ing on top of being silly. But, when Abby swallowed her mouthful and then opened her eyes to meet Euan's gaze, anything odd about what he was feeling vanished. The kick of physical desire was easy to recognise. And even more irresistible than the lure of Cath's cooking.

'That was *so* good…' Abby licked her lips.

It was just as well there was a large team of people working in the kitchen or he might have given in to the almost overwhelming desire to kiss her senseless, right here, right now—especially when he was pretty sure he might be seeing a similar desire in Abby's eyes. Then it occurred to him that as soon as they left the kitchen, they would be heading for a part of the castle that would be completely deserted, which was the only incentive he needed to break that eye contact and get moving.

'Thanks, Cath. You're a legend.'

Euan helped himself and Abby to another sausage that they ate as he led the way past tables where trifles and jellies, sandwiches and savouries and all sorts of other party food were being created. He took Abby to the staircase that led to the old servants' quarters and then an even narrower one that went up into a vast attic space.

A space that was crowded with old furniture and cobwebs, strange items like a dressmaker's dummy and a spinning wheel and many, many boxes full of things like books and vinyl records and toys and tea sets. Abby was wide-eyed as she looked around the dimly lighted space.

Any plan to steal a kiss had to be put aside, Euan decided, because Abby was far more interested in this treasure trove of discarded possessions.

'How on earth did anyone get those brass bed ends up those stairs? And, good grief— is that a *harp* over there?'

Euan shook his head. 'It's a nightmare I've been avoiding for a long time.'

'What is?'

'What to do about clearing this place when it comes time to sell the castle.'

'Sell?' Abby looked bewildered. 'Why would you do that?'

'There's no one other than me to inherit this place when...' Euan didn't want to finish his sentence. He didn't want to think about what was hanging over their heads this Christmas. That it could be Maggie's last.

'The boxes with the dress up costumes should be easy enough to find,' he said crisply. 'They get brought out and put back every year. Goodness knows why, when there's any number of empty rooms in more convenient places. I think my grandmother just likes to do things the way they've always been done. Have a look inside just to make sure we're not carrying anything downstairs that we won't need.'

Abby was quiet as she followed the direction he took towards a stack of cardboard cartons and he had the feeling she knew perfectly well why he'd changed the subject so abruptly. She could probably guess why he would never want to live here again or take on the running of this castle because she knew exactly how devastating the memories were. She'd seen him cry, for goodness' sake, and nobody had *seen* him cry since his daddy had died when he was seven.

Remembering that moment brought a rush of what were flashes of feeling rather than any coherent thoughts. Like the way he'd felt when Abby had thrown her arms around him when she'd seen those tears. When she'd quietly held him for as long as he'd needed it. And when she'd touched him later, as if she not only could anticipate what it was that he craved but that she wanted nothing more than to provide it.

And now, she was allowing the conversation to drift and let him escape what was too hard to think about before he was forced to.

'Traditions are important,' Abby said, as if that had been what they'd been discussing all along. 'Especially Christmas traditions. And I have a new one now, thanks to you.'

'Oh?' For a crazy moment Euan thought

she might be referring to their time together last night. It couldn't possibly become a Christmas tradition for either of them when their lives were going to head in completely different directions, probably on opposite sides of the globe, in a couple of days but, just for a nanosecond, he couldn't help thinking that kissing under the mistletoe or making love to Abby Hawkins at Christmas time would be a tradition that nothing could beat. Making love to her at any time of the year would be a gift…

Abby sighed happily as she crouched to open the top of a large box and check its contents. 'Yep. It won't be Christmas for me from now on without those pigs in blankets. I'm going to have to find out exactly how Cath makes them. Oh…' She lifted what was on top of the box. 'How cute is this?'

She stood up to hold a brown onesie with a white bib against her body. 'Darn. I think it's too small for me. Look, it's even got a hood with ears and antlers. Oh…oh, *yes*…' She dived back into the box. 'This is definitely me.'

She was slipping her arms into the elastic loops that were attached to a pair of angel wings. Then she folded the reindeer onesie and put it back into the box that she picked up. 'Where does it go?' she asked Euan.

'Put it over by the top of the stairs for now. We'll stack everything there before we start moving them. That way we shouldn't leave anything behind.'

He watched her walk past him towards the staircase, the single bulb hanging above her making those wings glimmer. Shiny, golden wings on either side of the fall of that magnificent mane of golden waves. Euan's fingers tingled as he remembered the way they'd buried themselves in that silky softness and he found himself taking in a slow, deep breath as he remembered the scent of her hair. His gaze was still fixed on Abby as she put the box down and turned back.

'What? Have I put it in the wrong place?'

'No. That's fine.'

Abby's eyebrows were raised in a silent question as she came closer.

'I was just thinking,' Euan admitted, 'that you suit those angel wings. When I first saw you in that pharmacy in Inverness, with your long, blonde hair and blue eyes, you looked like the kind of Christmas angels that people love to put on top of their trees.'

Abby's eyebrows went even higher. 'Coming from you, when we both know what you think of Christmas, I'm not sure that's a compliment.'

'Oh… I can assure you that it is.'

Abby was still walking towards him. She was close enough to touch. Close enough to kiss. All those flashes of feeling that Euan had just been aware of seemed to be coalescing into something bigger. Something so huge that it was more than disconcerting. This was alarming. He knew what big feelings could do to you. He'd made sure he'd never let it happen again. When he lost his beloved grandmother, that would be the end of it. There'd be no more people who'd been given his heart and were part of his soul. He'd be entirely alone in the world. Safer from emotional trauma than he'd ever been in his life.

The way he was feeling in this moment, however, was a threat to that safety. Part of Euan wanted to take a step back but it was too late. Abby was right in front of him, smiling up at him as she stood on tiptoes, offering him that kiss that had been hanging in the air from several steps back. And, like the way he'd thought she could see right through him, it seemed like she could sense his alarm.

'I could be a Christmas angel,' she said softly. 'Which would make me the absolute opposite of a Christmas puppy.'

It was Euan's turn to look bewildered.

'Because you can have me.' Abby was smiling now. 'But not for ever—just for Christmas.'

The light brush of her lips again his made Euan want to sink into a real kiss. The kind of kiss they'd shared last night so many times. The kind that made the outside world disappear. He was starting to feel safe again. What did it matter if he was thinking weird things about wanting more time with Abby so that he could do things to make her happy? It was never going to happen. They had a couple of days to share and that would be that.

'I know you don't believe in it.' Abby's lips were so close to his own that he could feel the movement of her words. 'But I think this is a bit of Christmas magic. Something that we're both going to remember every Christmas time for the rest of our lives.' He felt her breath now, as a sigh against his lips. 'I think remembering might become another tradition for me. You know, like pigs in blankets.'

And that did it. It wrapped up whatever it was between them as a physical pleasure in the same way that eating something delicious was. You could choose to do it, or not. You could indulge on special occasions. It was never going to control your life or be some kind of threat. It was safe, that was what it was. In a few days, Abby would be getting on with her life. She would no doubt head back to the land of sunshine and beaches for Christmas. She would find that man who was going to be the father of all those children he would never want himself. But she would remember the magic of her Christmas in Scotland.

Her Christmas with him.

It was almost a duty, wasn't it? To make that memory the best it could possibly be?

The angel wings were in the way of sliding his hands around Abby and pulling her body against his own while he kissed her senseless but maybe it was better this way, anyway—cupping her chin gently with one hand and threading his other hand under her hair to steady the back of her head—because kissing someone senseless required a bit of effort.

The responsive pressure of Abby's lips and the way they parted to allow the tip of her tongue to meet his made it very clear that this gorgeous woman was up for the challenge. The way Euan's thoughts were evaporating so that he was falling into this kiss to the exclusion of anything else made him wonder if he was the one who was going to end up senseless instead. Then he heard the tiny sound of bliss that came from Abby and he let go of any anxiety.

They were both heading in exactly the same direction.

And Abby had been right. It *was* a bit of magic.

CHAPTER EIGHT

ON THE MORNING of Christmas Eve, Abby was taking just a little longer with the children's medical checks. She didn't want to miss anything that might mean someone could miss out on the excitement of the building anticipation later today or the early hours of the big day itself.

The blue tinge to Callum's lips was a concern but, sadly, it was normal for him now. Abby increased the rate of oxygen being delivered through his nasal cannula and had to be satisfied when the saturation level went up even a little. There was no worrying change to his weight or heart rate or any other signs or symptoms that might indicate a worsening or imminently dangerous level of heart failure.

'Thank you for taking such good care of Callum,' his mum said to Abby as she wheeled his chair out of the treatment room. 'We're so happy to be here. And he just loved dressing up as an elf at the party last night. I've got photos that we're going to treasure for ever.'

'I know.' Abby gave her a hug. 'I'm collecting some of those myself.'

Like the one of Liam helping Lucy post her letter to Father Christmas in the forest. And one she'd taken last night, when she'd caught Euan sitting on a window seat in the corner of the drawing room, well away from the main entertainment being put on for the children and guests from the village. He'd had a *whole* plate of pigs in blankets on his lap, no doubt nicked from the buffet spread in the dining room. Not only that, but he'd been sharing the profits from his crime with Liam, who was sitting beside him. They were both watching what was going on and no doubt Liam was keeping a close eye on Lucy, but it was the matching expression on their faces that had prompted Abby to take the photo. That deep scowl. That look that said they might be doing their duty and turning up but they weren't about to let themselves enjoy this party. It had made Abby smile but then catch her breath as she felt that rush of heart-squeezing warmth that was as golden as those angel wings that she had been wearing in the attic and that Lucy had chosen to wear for the party. It was the feeling of love, that was what it was.

She'd paused to take a slow breath when she looked at the photo she'd just taken because something else was so obvious in the image. Maybe it was just the similar expressions but they looked so alike they could be father and son. What a shame he never wanted to have any children of his own, she thought, remembering how brilliantly Euan had handled the incident of the vanishing bagpipes, which could have made Liam's stay at the castle an ordeal that might confirm his mistrust of any adults for many years to come. He would have made an amazing father.

Milo also passed his check up this morning with flying colours. He'd been dressed up as a snowman last evening, which was a bit ironic after the fright he'd given them all while building one, but that black top hat had suited him perfectly and he'd made everybody laugh, himself most of all, by lifting it from his head and replacing it every time someone looked at or spoke to him.

'Did I see you eating two jellies at the

same time?' Abby asked as she recorded his weight. 'Red *and* green?'

Milo grinned at her and rubbed his belly and Abby had to return the smile. 'They were good, weren't they?'

'He was asleep the second his head hit the pillow,' Louise told her. 'All that excitement. I don't know where Maggie finds all that local talent. Who knew that the butcher was so good at making balloon animals?'

'Mmm.' Abby had her stethoscope against Milo's chest now so had an excuse not to respond but the truth was she'd barely noticed the balloon reindeers being produced. The whole party had been a bit of a blur, to be honest, because, after that time in the attic with Euan, and those mind-blowing kisses, Abby had been in such a state of anticipation about what she was quite confident was going to happen later that night that it was the main memory she'd been left with. Especially given that what *had* happened later last night had entirely lived up to those ridiculously high expectations.

Not just on a physical level. The touch and response of that oh, so private conversation between lovers and the joy to be found in both the build up and the ultimate release had been equally one of emotion, at least for Abby. She was quietly sure that it had been something more than purely physical for Euan, too. Why else would he have held her as she slept until the early hours of this morning, when he'd finally slipped out of her bed to go back to his own room?

Abby hadn't gone back to sleep. She had lain in that wonderful old bed and realised she was missing him already. She knew this couldn't last. She'd been completely sincere when she'd told Euan that the pleasure of indulging the astonishing attraction they had discovered between them was just for Christmas and not for ever, but she knew she had offered that reassurance because she sensed he was about to run—to repair all those defensive barriers of his and to even try to add an extra layer of safety.

Good grief…this was a man who'd convinced himself, decades ago, that opening his heart to anyone was a path straight to unbearable emotional distress. And, while Abby might be someone who was simply passing through his life briefly, she also represented his worst nightmare—a woman who couldn't wait to start creating as big a family as she possibly could and who loved celebrating every aspect of Christmas as much as his grandmother did. Abby had recognised that Euan was the total opposite of anybody she would consider suitable as a life partner and that had to work both ways. Which meant that she was the equivalent of a 'bad girl' for this taciturn and no doubt normally extremely well-behaved Scotsman.

She rather liked that idea.

What Abby didn't like was the change she found in Lucy, who was her last patient to check. The little girl was so pale but still found a gorgeous smile for Abby when Maggie brought her over to the clinic. She was still wearing the angel wings and pretty, white dress that had been her party costume.

'I'm an angel,' she told Abby.

'You are the most beautiful angel ever.'

'Liam said I couldn't wear them because it wasn't the party any more.'

'And I said she could keep them,' Maggie said. 'And wear them whenever she wants to. I'm not sure how happy Liam was about that, though.'

'He doesn't like dressing up much, does he?'

'He doesn't like pretend,' Lucy agreed. 'He says it makes real too hard.'

Abby and Maggie exchanged a glance that was a silent conversation in an instant. The wisdom of a child and the sadness that Lucy's brother already found life so hard.

'But I love pretend,' Lucy added. 'I want to be a princess, really. But now I love being an angel, too.'

'Well, let's pop you on the scales, Princess Lucy.' Abby held out her hand. 'I want to see how much you ate at the party.'

Not that food had anything to do with the increase in Lucy's weight. Or the crackling sounds in the base of her lungs or the fact that her blood oxygen levels had dipped overnight.

'I'm not happy,' Abby told Euan a short time later, when she went back to the castle and went over the details of her examination with him. 'I've already increased her diuretics to get rid of that extra fluid and we could maybe give her a bit of supplementary oxygen, which might well be all that's needed, but I'd be a lot happier with some more information. I'd like to know what her ventricular function and blood flow is looking like and what her ejection fraction is. Most of all, I'd like to be able to rule out a complication like a thrombosis.'

She broke off abruptly as Maggie came into the foyer with Lucy, who immediately dropped Maggie's hand and ran towards Abby, who swept her up into her arms for a cuddle, taking care not to squash the angel wings. Even with that short burst of energy Lucy was a little out of breath and Abby caught Euan's gaze as she held the little girl close.

'I know it's Christmas Eve, and probably impossible, but could you find out whether your friend could organise an echo and even an MRI if it's indicated?'

'I'll ring him and find out. I'm happy to take her into Inverness if they can make it happen.'

'You'll need to take Liam with you as well,' Abby said. 'He would be distraught if Lucy was taken off to hospital without him.'

Catching Maggie's gaze now, Abby re-alised that it had to be obvious she was going to be worried sick herself. It had to be just as clear how tightly Lucy was clinging to her. Was she aware that people were worried and wanted to both offer and receive comfort? Abby pressed a kiss to those gorgeous red curls. Lucy was the sweetest child she'd ever met. How could anyone spend time with her and not fall completely in love?

'You'll need some help with two children and a hospital appointment to juggle.' Maggie's expression was impossible to read. 'Take Abby with you.'

'But that would leave you without a doctor available.'

'Graham will be happy to come to the castle,' Maggie responded. 'He can deal with any emergency and call for extra help if it's needed. Plus, it'll give him a chance to lecture me at the same time. Oh…' Maggie turned her head as she began to walk away with the kind of step that advertised the need to organise something. 'You can do me a favour while you're in town. Just a couple of last-minute things on my shopping list. If all goes well, you could have a treat for lunch, perhaps, and let the children see what's going on in the high street on your way home while you sort that out for me.'

The echocardiography room might be very dim to allow the images on the screen to be more easily interpreted but Euan could read the expression on Liam's face all too well. Maybe he should have suggested that he waited outside with Liam while Abby and his friend Mike, the cardiologist in Inverness, watched the Doppler ultrasound examination of Lucy's heart.

Except that it had been all too easy to read what was going on in his head then, as well. Too easy to imagine that this was himself at ten years old, about to be separated from his sister while she had a test that could be frightening or painful.

So they all went in. Abby was holding Lucy's hand and making sure the little girl stayed as still as possible as she lay on the bed, wearing the angel wings she'd refused to take off.

'I'm an angel,' she'd told the technician. 'Angels can't take off their wings.'

'Of course they can't, darling. I knew that.'

Abby's eyes were glued to the screen now where colours and shapes shifted and changed and her conversation with the cardiologist was calm and quiet.

Euan and Liam stood to one side and they were far enough away for anything they said to not interfere with the examination.

'Have you seen a Doppler ultrasound test before, Liam?'

A jerky head shake was the only response

Euan got. He could actually feel how tensely this lad was holding himself.

'It doesn't hurt. That device the technician is using is called a transducer and it can send and receive sound waves. It can see blood moving because the movement changes the pitch of the reflected sounds.'

It could also detect blood that had stopped moving completely and become a dangerous clot, which Euan knew was top of the list of Abby's concerns. Not that he was about to let Liam know that. The small voice beside him was a welcome distraction to even thinking about unwanted complications for Lucy.

'Is it like what dolphins use?'

'Bit more like bats than dolphins but it's kind of complicated. I'll try and explain later if you want.'

Liam shrugged and lapsed into silence, which meant that Euan could hear what Mike and Abby were saying.

'That's a good apical four-chamber view.'

'It's looking good. I hope we're not wasting your time. Seems like the change we've made to Lucy's diuretic therapy is already clearing any extra fluid that was interfering with her oxygen uptake. I just…wanted to be extra sure.'

'It's not a problem. I'd feel the same way.'

'Can we get a right ventricle ejection fraction from end-systolic and end-diastolic volumes?'

'Of course...'

Everybody was focused on the shifting colours and shapes on the screen as the technician worked.

'What are the different colours?' Liam whispered to Euan. 'Is red good or bad?'

'The red is the blood that has oxygen in it and the blue is the blood where it's all used up so it needs to go to the lungs and get some new oxygen.' But Euan could sense that Liam was lost already and he could feel something like a kick in his gut. Had nobody ever sat down with this boy and explained exactly what was wrong with his sister's heart?

Maybe he'd known too much himself but it had helped. So had being included in discussions and treated like an extra adult in Fi's support team.

'You know that a normal heart has two sides?' he asked Liam. 'The right and the left?'

'I guess.'

'And with people like Lucy, the left side doesn't grow properly and it can't pump blood around the body so things need to be switched around. The blood gets sent to the lungs in a different way and the good ventricle can take over the job of pumping the blood with the oxygen in it to all the places it needs to go. I've got some good pictures somewhere. I could find them for you.'

Liam nodded. 'Okay.'

He could tell him, Euan thought. About Fiona. Tell him that he understood what it was like for Liam because he could remember how lonely it was to feel as if he were the only boy in the world with a problem this big. Except he didn't know exactly what it was like, did he? He hadn't had to be forcibly separated from his sister while she was still alive. He'd been allowed to be involved every step of the way with her care. He'd been allowed to love her with every breath he took.

It was his turn to lapse into silence as the examination continued. He tuned in to what was being said and it was obvious that they were all happy with what they were seeing. The blood flow was exactly as it should be and the amount being ejected from the heart with every beat was within an acceptable range to allow for Lucy to be engaging in normal activities. The tricuspid valve was functioning well and there was no sign of any clots in the vessels, heart chambers or lungs.

Mike shook Abby's hand as the examination was completed. 'I wish we had someone with your training available here,' he told her. 'I'd love to do that course you've just finished but there's no way I can get away from here for something like that. Not when we're short-staffed as it is.'

'Thank you so much for fitting us in on Christmas Eve. It's such a relief to know that Princess Lucy is good to go.'

Mike ruffled Lucy's curls. 'Merry Christmas, Princess.'

'Can we go now?' Liam asked. 'You said we could have burgers for lunch.'

'I did,' Euan agreed. He caught Abby's gaze. 'If that's okay with you?'

'Are you kidding? I *love* burgers.' She was bundling Lucy into her pink coat. 'Let's go. We've got those messages to do for Maggie, as well.'

'So...did that burger live up to expectations?'

'It was *so* good.' Abby beamed at Euan. She reached for a couple of stray, now-cold French fries and ate those as well.

Euan shook his head. Only Abby Hawkins

could look this happy about being in a fast-food restaurant, eating junk food, amongst the absolute chaos of last-minute shopping in the main street of Inverness. Very close to the pharmacy where their paths had crossed for the first time, in fact, in what now seemed like a life-changing moment in time for Euan McKendry. He knew that there were some things he'd never see in quite the same light again. Like long blonde hair. And golden angel wings like the ones Lucy was still wearing, one a little bent after she'd been lying on it at the hospital, as she let Liam push her on the swing in the restaurant's play area.

She *was* a wee angel. Euan watched as Lucy tipped her head back to grin at her big brother as he let go of the swing. He could hear her laughter even through the infernal din all the other children were making in this overcrowded space and it was pulling him back to how he'd felt wondering about whether to tell Liam about *his* sister. How it felt as if the pull into the past was getting too strong. Too fraught with painful memories that were shifting and changing, like the images of Lucy's heart on the screen, but these were somewhere very deep in Euan's heart. The sooner they got out of here, the better.

'We should go,' he said to Abby. 'I just need to pop into the bagpipe shop for something and we can head home.'

Home…

Funny thing, given that he hadn't lived at the castle for nearly two decades, but it really did feel like that was what they would be doing when they left. Heading home.

'I'd like to go back to that pharmacy.' Abby seemed to be making an effort to keep a straight face. 'I seem to have misplaced my elf headband.'

Euan wanted to shake his head again but, instead, he let his mouth curl into a bit of a smile. He'd hated that headband with such a passion, hadn't he? And yet, that was something else he'd see differently from now on because Abby had shown him that there was a place for silliness at Christmas. For smiles and laughter and joy that was safe enough to take pleasure from because you knew it was temporary. Just for Christmas.

'Oh…' he said aloud. 'We need to get that toy dog. For Leah. Come on, let's get cracking. I think there's a store down the road that has lots of toys.'

Abby buttoned Lucy into her warm, bright pink coat, cleverly shifting the elastic loops of her wings so she didn't have to take them off. Then there were the woolly hat and mittens, which took extra time because a cuddle was needed. Euan and Liam had put their puffer jackets and hats on and were waiting near the door where an older woman was clearing a table and wiping it down. She paused to watch Abby and Lucy join them and she gave them all a misty smile.

'You have the most adorable children,' she told them. 'And I hope you have such a happy Christmas.'

Abby looked startled for a moment and then almost guilty as she realised they'd been taken for a family. She avoided Euan's gaze as she smiled brightly back at the woman.

'You too,' she said warmly. 'Merry Christmas.'

'I'm an angel,' Lucy told her.

'That you are, pet.'

Euan just grunted. So did Liam.

But something caught in his chest as he held the door for Abby and the children to go out ahead of him. Something so big it was impossible to breathe around. This was like the fantasy of letting himself get as close as he had to Abby, wasn't it?

But this was an even bigger fantasy. Of a whole family, including Abby.

But just for Christmas.

And that made it okay for Euan to tell Abby to take the children with her to the pharmacy to find another elf headband and they would meet at the toy shop in ten minutes or so. He would go to the bagpipe shop alone, to find a book of simple tunes for a learner to play on a practice chanter. He might have a look at the chanters they had available as well, because Liam would not only need one of his own after he went home, a child-sized one would be easier. He would make sure he found some time later today to give the lad another lesson, too, because Euan knew that the busier he kept himself, the better, because it filled the spaces where things he didn't want to think about could sneak into his head.

Oh, *man*…

That look on the woman's face when she'd told them they had the most adorable children. When she'd assumed that they were a family.

Abby already knew that she had fallen in love with Euan and that it was just a few days of living a fantasy but this had just taken it to a completely different dimension. *This* was the real fantasy. Not just a gorgeous man and amazing sex and a Christmas to die for. This was what Abby had been searching for. This feeling of family. She was with a man she was in love with and children she'd also fallen for.

And yes, she still knew perfectly well that it was the last thing Euan would want and had to carefully avoid even catching his gaze, but Abby intended to hang onto this feeling. To memorise it perfectly, because then she would recognise it when she found it again. If she was lucky enough to find it again.

The pharmacy had sold out of elf headbands but there was a halo that was the finishing touch Lucy needed for her angel impersonation and the joy on Lucy's face earned a grateful glance from Liam. He almost smiled but grunted instead and it was so like Euan that Abby not only had to fight the urge to pull him close for a hug, she also had to blink back tears.

They got back to the castle a bit after two o'clock, after a somewhat rushed visit to the toy shop, when the rest of the children were settling in for the quiet time after lunch. Like last night, they all needed to save their energy for something special that evening— this time for the carol singing in Kirkwood's picturesque stone church in the village.

Maggie seemed very happy to see them back, to hear the good news about the results of Lucy's examination and collect the shopping they'd done for her, but there was something that didn't feel quite right. When Abby had tucked Lucy into bed for a nap, promising to come back and check on her soon, she hurried back down the stairs having come to the conclusion that Maggie was hiding something.

She found Euan coming out of the drawing room.

'Is Maggie in there?'

'No. She's not in the kitchens, either. She's probably in the library.'

Abby held his gaze. 'So, you felt it, too? She's hiding something, isn't she?'

'I just spoke to the GP, Graham. He said he'd rung about the results of her biopsy, hoping they might have come back.'

Abby's heart sank like a stone. 'And they have?'

'Apparently so. He wouldn't tell me, though. He said that was my grandmother's business.'

Their shared glance became a pact. They were both going to find out what was going on. Maggie was in the library, sitting behind a huge desk in one corner of the book-lined room. Euan and Abby kept moving until they were standing in front of it but, as Abby waited for Euan to ask the question, she realised that he was scared stiff and her heart broke for him. He didn't want to know the answer, did he, in case it meant the beginning of the end?

Abby moved sideways. Just enough for her hand to be touching Euan's and, as if it was an automatic response, his fingers curled around hers. It was Abby who cleared her throat carefully.

'We've heard that you've had some news about your biopsy,' she said quietly. 'Would you rather talk to Euan alone?'

Maggie blinked and then her face softened as she let her gaze settle on her grandson. 'Oh, lovie. I'm sorry. I'd almost forgotten about that news. And it's good. The tumour's not malignant. I'm going to need surgery as soon as possible in the new year but... I'm not going to die. Well, not just yet, anyway.'

Abby's hand was being gripped so hard her fingers were going numb. It was very revealing that Euan could hide such an emotional response by speaking so calmly.

'That *is* good news, Gammy. The best Christmas gift I could have wished for.'

Abby extracted her hand from Euan's so that she could go to the other side of the desk and throw her arms around Maggie. She had tears in her eyes, and so did Maggie, but the difference was that Maggie was looking anything but happy.

'What is it?' Abby asked, frowning, as something that Maggie had said earlier clicked into place. 'What was it that made you almost forget about such amazing news?'

'Judith rang.' Maggie had to pause and take a deep, shaky breath.

'Oh, no… Has her father died?'

'No. In fact, he's doing better than expected after surgery. That's not what she called about.'

'What is it?'

Maggie closed her eyes for a long beat as she started speaking again. 'They've found a new foster home for Lucy. Someone who's had a CHD child in the past and knows exactly what they're signing up for. It sounds perfect.' She opened her eyes but avoided looking up and her voice was still strained. 'A woman who lives right beside a beautiful beach but only a few minutes from a hospital that has a specialty paediatric cardiac unit. And she breeds Shetland ponies and...and...'

'It does sound perfect,' Euan said.

'But it's not, is it?'

Abby's question was more a quiet statement and Maggie shook her head in agreement. 'She can't—or won't—consider taking Liam. Apparently she fostered a boy about his age once and it was a bit of a catastrophe. I've said that he's a wonderful lad and just needs the reassurance that he can stay with his sister. It's possible that a meeting could be arranged, but...'

'But that's not really going to help, is it?' Euan's breath came out in a heavy sigh. 'And why would he try to pretend that he won't make any trouble? He has good reason not to trust anyone.'

'We can't tell him,' Maggie said. 'Not yet. Let them at least have a Christmas Day they can remember as being together and happy.'

She brushed away a tear from her cheek. 'It might well be their last one.'

Abby straightened as she caught a movement from the corner of her eye. Her head turned sharply towards the door, in time to see someone stepping back.

'Liam? Is that you?'

But the figure had vanished. Abby exchanged an alarmed glance with Euan.

'I sent him to find the practice chanter in my bagpipe case,' he said, the frown lines deepening around his eyes. 'I was going to give him a lesson while Lucy had her nap. He might have come looking for me.'

'How long do you think he was there?' Maggie sounded as horrified as they were all feeling. 'How much could he have heard?'

Euan's voice was grim. 'If he heard any of what we were saying, it would have been too much. I'd better go and have a talk to him.' He turned on his heel to leave.

'And I'll go and check on Lucy,' Abby said. But she paused to give Maggie another hug. 'Are you okay?'

'Those poor wee bairns.' Maggie wiped her eyes. 'They remind me so much of Euan when he was a lad. And our wee Fi, of course.' The sadness in her eyes as she looked up at Abby was unbearable.

'We can't let it happen,' Abby said. 'There must be something we can do to stop them being separated like this.'

But Maggie shook her head. 'I'd adopt them myself in a heartbeat,' she said. 'But I know they wouldn't consider me. Not at my age and with the health issues I've got ahead of me.' The strength that Abby had sensed in this woman from the moment she'd met her seemed to be fading away. 'Lucy needs someone a lot younger than me to be her mother.'

'She needs to be with her brother, too. She needs Liam as much as he needs her.'

And Abby needed to go and stand in that bedroom door and just watch the little girl sleep for a moment. Or to tiptoe into the room and leave a butterfly's kiss on those curls. In the end, however, she did neither of those things. Seconds after she went up that grand staircase with its bannisters woven with Christmas decorations, she was running back down. Euan was moving almost as fast as he came out of the drawing room.

'I can't find him,' Euan said. 'And nobody's seen him.' He held his hands up in a gesture of helplessness. 'This place is so big. He could be anywhere...'

Abby's mouth was so dry it was hard to speak. 'Lucy's gone, too,' she told him. 'Her bed's still warm but...it's empty...'

CHAPTER NINE

EVERY AVAILABLE ADULT was called in to help with the search. Catherine the cook simply turned off the ovens and abandoned the sponge cakes she'd been baking for afternoon tea. Ben's grandma and Ruth were left in charge of all the children who were engaged in quiet activities in the drawing room and Callum's mum was watching over a few sleeping children including her own. Every other parent, caregiver and volunteer helper dispersed all over the castle and outbuildings in a commendably short space of time.

'Should we call for more help?' Maggie asked anxiously. 'Like the police?'

'Not yet,' Euan said. 'But you could call the Kirkwood station and let them know what's happening so they're on standby. If we haven't found them within an hour, we'll be in trouble. It'll be starting to get dark by then and we'll need to activate an official search and rescue with dogs, maybe.'

In the meantime, they needed to cover as much ground as they could.

'Where should we go?' Abby watched Maggie head outside, already talking on her phone, presumably to a member of the local police force. 'Somewhere that isn't being covered already.'

'Let me think for a moment…' Euan found it easy to put himself in Liam's place. He could imagine himself at ten years old, desperate to stop anyone taking his sister away from him. He could guess where he might go to hide in this vast, old house as well, but then he had the advantage of knowing pretty much every square inch of it.

'One thing we can be certain about,' he said to Abby, 'is that Liam won't be heading anywhere that he'd think an adult might be. So he's not likely to go to the stable conversion where the clinic is even though we've still got people checking there.'

'He might have gone to the stables where the animals are, though. Lucy loves those donkeys.'

'That's where Gammy's gone,' Euan reminded her. 'I'm going to head up the back staircase first. It's lucky that we've got areas closed off and locked in other parts of the castle, but there are all those old bedrooms as well as the staircase up to the attic that it's easy to get to and it would be the kind of place I would have gone at his age.'

'I'm coming with you.'

Euan didn't argue. There was no point in sending Abby off in another direction because she didn't know the castle layout as well as he did. Besides, they all knew how attached Lucy was to Abby. If the little girl was going to respond to anyone's call, it would be Abby's. And, on a selfish note, Euan wanted her company. Because a fear he thought he'd banished for ever was beginning to surface and he really didn't want to be left without the escape of being able to distract himself.

It took several minutes to open all the doors to small, disused bedrooms and bathrooms in the rabbit warren of the old servants' quarters and there was no sign of Liam or Lucy. It was another minute or two to get back to the staircase that led up to the attic and, the moment they got up there, they could sense the emptiness of the space.

'Lucy? Are you in here, sweetheart?' Abby's voice echoed in the vast area. 'Lucy? *Liam...?*'

She caught Euan's gaze as the echo faded into a dense silence. And then she held the eye contact for a heartbeat longer. Was she having the same flash of remembering what had happened the last time they were alone in this space? Those heady kisses? That silent pact they'd made to make the most of the magic they'd found together because it was only ever going to be for Christmas? Not that it mattered now. Nothing mattered except to find Liam and Lucy. That they were safe.

Euan turned away from the intense scrutiny he'd been giving the attic space even though his gut had instantly told him it was empty of everything except junk and dust.

'They're not here.'

'Let's go downstairs again. Maybe someone else has found them.'

Euan shook his head. 'I've got my phone. Maggie would let me know.'

His grandmother was probably feeling as sick as he was at this turn of events. If only they hadn't been talking about the children. If only Liam hadn't overheard the plan to destroy the part of his world that mattered the most. If only he and Maggie didn't know exactly how scared Liam had to be feeling right now, knowing that the worst was going to happen and that he had absolutely no control over it.

It was instinctive to head to where Maggie was searching. Just to touch base and make sure that she was coping. Even with the immense relief of knowing that Maggie didn't have a malignancy that could have meant she had very little time left, she was still unwell, in pain, and facing major surgery. At nearly eighty years old, she really didn't need this extra stress. It was hard enough having these two children here, like small ghosts of their own pasts. That something terrible could happen while they were here at the castle was…well, it was unthinkable.

Euan pulled open the massive front door. Again, he had one of those unwelcome flashbacks that were entirely irrelevant right now. This time, it was the shock of opening this door to find the Christmas angel from the pharmacy on his doorstep. Wearing that ridiculous headband with the elf on it, the joy of the season still shining in her eyes.

There was no joy in her voice behind him right now.

'Oh, no…'

He spun around. 'What?'

'Lucy's coat. I left it on that table when we got back. With her hat. It's not there.'

They stared at each other for a long moment, as the horror sank in that their search area might be expanding exponentially. That they might have hypothermia to add to any concerns for the children's safety because it was beginning to snow again. Just a gentle drift of flakes but it could get heavier at any time.

'There'll be footprints,' Abby said. 'In the snow. And...' She closed her eyes as if summoning a memory that could be important. 'There's only one path that Liam knows about—the one we took in the sleigh, to go to the letter box tree.'

'Get your coat.' Euan's instruction came out in a snap of urgency. 'And hat. I'll meet you in the kitchen garden.'

Only a minute or two later and they were off on their new search, buttoning their jackets as they moved. It was hard to tell if there were any fresh footprints in the snow after the activities of building the snowman and the sleigh ride and the marks that were there were already being softened by new flakes, but Abby's guess as to where Liam might have taken his sister was as good as any to go on and there were already other people fanning out from the castle in different directions.

They raced past the snowman with his carrot nose and forked branches for arms and hands and into the forest, following the same track the sleigh had taken. Was it only yesterday he'd been walking this path, alongside Leah's dad, talking about how looking after a dog could give her both companionship and confidence? He'd surprised himself by enjoying the outing, hadn't he? And Abby had looked so happy up there in the sleigh with Lucy snuggled on her lap and Liam hunched beside her.

'What were you and Liam talking about in the sleigh yesterday? He was pointing at something.'

'He could see the lake through the trees. We were talking about going ice skating but that we didn't know if it was safe enough yet.' Abby cupped her hands around her mouth. 'Lucy,' she called. '*Liam?* Please come out. *Please*...' She bit her lip, turning her head to scan in all directions. 'Lucy's coat is so bright. Surely we'd catch a glimpse through the trees, even if they were trying to hide.'

Euan stopped in his tracks.

'What is it?'

'The rowboat.'

'Out on the lake? Near the mistletoe tree? What about it?'

'It's big enough to hide in if you're small. It's about the only thing out here that is.' Without thinking, he held out his hand and Abby took it with no hesitation at all. They didn't even need to speak to know exactly what they were both thinking and they both began moving in the same instant, running through the trees, taking the quickest route to the lake that they could. Euan could feel the warmth of her hand even through two layers of woollen gloves. More than that, he could feel the same desperation he had, to find these two children before anything terrible happened. It felt almost as if he were looking after Fiona all over again. That this was *his* responsibility.

There were footprints at the edge of the lake in snow that hadn't been trampled by many feet. And they were too small to have been made by the wellington boots he and Abby had been wearing on their mission to gather mistletoe.

'Liam?' Euan's voice seemed to bounce

off the expanse of ice in front of them. It sounded loud. And angry? He tried to soften his tone. 'Where are you?'

'Lucy?' Abby's voice also rang out like a bell. 'Where are you, princess? I need a cuddle.'

And then they saw it. A flash of pink as a small hand gripped the edge of the rowboat. A head popped up over the side and Lucy was smiling at them.

'We're hiding,' she said. 'It's a game. *Ouch...*' Lucy looked down. 'Don't pull me, Liam. I don't like it.'

Euan stepped out onto the ice. He got three steps in before he heard the loud crack and when he looked down, he could see a deep crack and smaller fractures spreading like a spider's web. He put his arm out to stop Abby coming onto the ice.

'Stay there,' he told her. 'It's not safe.'

'I'm not as heavy as you are. It might be okay for me.'

That wasn't a risk Euan was prepared to take. The urge to protect Abby was far too strong to ignore. He didn't want to risk falling into the lake himself, either, or creating holes that would endanger the children. He could spread his weight by lying down and rolling, or sliding towards the boat, and he might be able to bring Lucy back that way, but would Liam come back without a struggle? He knew all too well how desperate this lad was feeling. He also knew what was most important to him and maybe he could use that to get them both to safety.

'Talk to me, Liam,' he called. 'I need you to help us get Lucy back to somewhere warm. It's far too cold for her out here.'

Liam had to be lying on the bottom of the boat to remain invisible. His voice was clear enough, however. And it was angry.

'We're not coming back.'

'I want to go back.' Lucy was trying to stand up. 'I'm cold, Liam. And I'm hungry.'

'We can't go back, Luce.' Liam was speaking more quietly now.

'Why not?'

'We just can't.'

Euan exchanged a glance with Abby. At least Liam hadn't told Lucy what was going to happen after Christmas. If he did, they would have two distraught children to deal with. Abby would be just as upset, he thought, noting how pale and strained her face was.

'Liam?' It was Abby who called this time.

'I know what you're worried about and…it's not going to happen.'

Euan's jaw dropped. What was she doing?

'I won't let it happen,' Abby said firmly.

Euan closed his eyes as his heart sank. When he opened them again, Liam was sitting up in the boat, his gaze fixed on Abby.

'Really?' he asked. 'Do you promise?'

No…but Euan didn't say the word aloud. He couldn't be the one to shatter the hope he could see on this boy's face. The hope he could actually feel inside his own chest even though he knew it wasn't based on anything real. Surely he could trust that Abby wasn't about to make a promise she couldn't possibly keep? To give Liam even more hope that would only make the inevitable all the more devastating?

But his trust was obviously misplaced.

'I promise,' Abby said.

Okay…maybe the promise was a little premature because Abby hadn't done her homework yet but that didn't make it any less genuine. She *was* going to do whatever she could to make sure that this brother and sister stayed together.

The moment she'd seen Lucy's head bob

up over the side of that rowboat and had seen the smile that was already imprinted on her heart for ever, something came together and she just *knew*. That trip out with the children this morning had let her know that she'd found exactly what she wanted in life, in that feeling of family that being with Euan and the children had given her. She'd known all along that being with children was going to be a huge part of her future, both professionally and personally. She'd also known that she'd know what felt right when she found it. She'd learned to trust her instincts in matters such as this.

She had found it. And her heart was telling her it was the right thing. But it wasn't just any children, was it?

It was *these* children. Liam and Lucy. A damaged boy and a little girl who needed to cram a lifetime of love into who knew how long? Abby loved them both. With all her heart.

She loved Euan as well, but that was a completely different kind of love. And he didn't need saving.

Well…he actually did, but nobody could help him if he didn't want to be saved. And, right now, he was looking as if he didn't even want to be anywhere near Abby. He was looking…furious?

He was keeping it hidden, mind you, as he talked Liam into getting out of the boat and then lifting Lucy onto the ice. He coaxed Lucy into walking alone. 'You're as light as a feather,' he told her. 'It's quite safe.'

Lucy tiptoed across the ice until she got close to Euan.

'Go to Dr Abby,' he said. 'She's going to look after you.' Even his tone was so neutral Abby could tell it was being used to disguise what he was feeling. Maybe he was hiding it so well, he couldn't even see it himself.

But Lucy didn't continue on to where Abby was standing. She stayed where she was and smiled at Euan as she held her arms up.

You'd have to have a heart of stone to resist that plea but was Lucy aware of the hesitation before she was picked up? Or that Euan's face was definitely like stone as he walked towards Abby and transferred Lucy into her arms? He didn't even meet Abby's gaze.

'Your turn now, Liam,' he said, turning his back on Abby. 'But if you hear the ice cracking, you need to lie down, okay?'

Why was Euan so angry? Was he afraid

that she would expect him to be a part of the lives of these children as well? Was it too much of a pull back into the past for him? She could still hear the sadness in Maggie's voice.

'They remind me so much of Euan when he was a lad. And our wee Fi, of course…'

Abby could understand that. And it might break her heart to know that she'd never see Euan again, but she could live with it. After all, she hadn't expected anything more from him than this magical few days fate had somehow decreed they could have together.

What she couldn't live with would be turning her back on Liam and Lucy. Again, she could hear an echo of Maggie's voice.

'Lucy needs someone a lot younger than me to be her mother…'

She'd have Maggie on her side, she was quite sure of that. And, somehow, she was going to make this work. She had to, because she'd made a promise and she wasn't going to let Liam grow up to be like Euan and believe that Christmas was about promises that got made and then broken.

'I think it's a wonderful idea. Exactly what I would do if I was you, Abby.'

'It's a daft idea,' Euan snapped. 'Totally impractical.'

'For whom? Me?' Abby folded her arms. 'Isn't that something I get to decide for myself?'

Euan, Abby and Maggie were back in the library. This time, the door was not only firmly closed, Catherine the cook had been tasked with keeping the children in the kitchen and making their afternoon tea of hot chocolate and cookies last until someone came to get them.

'Do you not think I'd feel partly responsible if you throw away your career after an impulsive decision you make when you're in *my* home?'

'Why would I be throwing away my career?' There was a flash of defiance in Abby's eyes. 'Women with children can work as well as raise kids these days, you know. And I've already told you that having children in my life is important enough for me to work around the commitment. I could be happy working as a GP.'

'Oh…' Maggie's sigh was pure hope. 'We so need a new GP in Kirkwood.' Then she shook the distraction away. 'But we can talk about that later. As for you, Euan, this isn't really your home any more, is it? It's mine. You haven't lived here since you went to medical school. You don't even like coming back for Christmas, do you? You just do it because you think it's what I want.'

'That's not true.' Except that it kind of was—he just didn't like it to be spelled out. And it wasn't the whole truth. He did it because he loved his grandmother. It was a shock to hear the criticism that was almost anger in her voice. Gammy had never spoken to him like this.

'I'll support Abby in any way I can to foster and adopt these bairns,' Maggie continued. 'Whether or not she wants to take over from Graham. They can all live here. With me.'

Euan let out a careful breath. 'You can't do that, Gammy.'

'Don't tell me what I can or can't do, Euan.' Maggie raised her eyebrows. 'Last time I looked, this is my life, what's left of it.'

'Exactly. There won't be very much left of it if you take on a problem like these children.'

'Have I ever told you what you should do with *your* life?' Maggie was on her feet now, all five foot nothing of her. 'Have I said you should come and live here in the home that you grew up in that will be yours one of these days? No... I haven't. And I wouldn't, so don't you be doing it to me.' She was walking towards the door now but she paused before pulling it open to fire another volley over her shoulder. 'Or, heaven forbid, I could have told you that you should have let Graham retire years ago by coming home and being the GP that our village so badly needs. But did I do that? No, of course I didn't. Because I love you and because you're an adult and you get to make your own decisions.' She was half-way out of the door now but she raised her voice before slamming it shut behind her. 'Even if they're the *wrong* decisions.'

Abby was looking as shocked as Euan was feeling. Or maybe it was awkwardness that she had been drawn into family tensions that had been buried for decades. Tensions that had nothing to do with her. Except they did now, didn't they? And maybe Abby had just realised that she had triggered this unprecedented confrontation.

'I'm sorry, Euan,' she said. 'I didn't mean to cause trouble between you and your grandmother.'

Euan just stared at her. There was such

a mix of feelings going on in his head that it was too hard to find any words. He was upset that his grandmother was so upset. He was worried about her. He was worried about Lucy and Liam and…and, yes, he was worried about Abby as well. Maybe it had been an unwise choice to get so close to someone who was so different they would never be able to understand him but that didn't mean he didn't care about her. A lot more than he was comfortable caring for anyone. Enough that he couldn't let her throw her chance of a happy future away.

'You do realise how crazy this is, don't you? That you think you can swoop in like some guardian angel and fix the lives of two children you only met a couple of days ago?'

Oh, help…that reference to her being an angel had been a bad idea. It made him remember their first meeting. Worse, it made him remember how he'd felt when he saw her wearing the angel wings in the attic. About wanting to make Abby happy. Wanting to have more time with her. As much time as possible…

It was a catalyst to make the turbulent emotions he was grappling with unbearable and there was only one way out of this. To open that mental door, shove everything inside and slam it shut, the way Maggie had just slammed the library door shut. The easiest way to find the strength to do that was by harnessing a new emotion.

Anger.

'You actually made a promise to Liam and Lucy that you *were* going to fix their lives. Do you have any idea how unlikely it is that you're going to be able to keep that promise? I don't care how good your intentions might have been, to make a promise like that... a promise you probably can't even keep...it would be unforgivable at any time but...to do it at *Christmas*? When you knew they'd written that damn letter saying that was their Christmas wish? How *could* you?'

'I don't happen to think it's that unlikely.' Abby lifted her chin. Aye, she was really defiant now. And he had to admire how determined she sounded. 'I think that they'd see a paediatrician with specialist cardiology training as an ideal carer for Lucy. And I have support from someone who would make it even more of a family situation for them. I might just take up your grandmother's incredibly generous offer to live here.'

'You cannot do that.' Euan's face had frozen so hard he could barely get the words out.

'What? Live here at the castle with Maggie? Give up a career as a specialist consultant to be a GP? Become a mother to two children who need to be together more than anything else?' Abby was controlling her voice so well, her words were quiet but it was obvious she was as angry as Euan was feeling. 'Give everything I've got to love them as much as they deserve to be loved?' Her voice finally wobbled. '*All* of the above?'

'It would destroy you.'

'How can you be so sure about that?'

'Because, as we both know perfectly well, Lucy's not going to live for ever.'

Abby shook her head, dismissing his words. 'None of us are going to live for ever,' she said. The look she was giving Euan seemed almost one of pity. 'If you take the attitude that you're not going to love someone—or let them love you—because it's going to hurt when it's over, then…then you're not really living at all.' Abby looked as if she was going to follow Maggie's example and walk out on him. And yes, she was continuing to tell him what she thought as she turned away. 'I'm more than prepared to risk the heartbreak of loving,' she told him. 'Because that's the only way to find the joy.' She shook her head again. 'I feel sorry for you. You're never going to feel that joy again, are you?'

'It will destroy you,' Euan said again. 'Like it destroyed my mother.'

That stopped her. She turned back. Blinked. Took a long, slow inward breath.

'Tell me,' she said quietly. 'What did happen to your mother? Why does nobody talk about it?'

'Maybe it was one tragedy too many. Or maybe we feel responsible in some way.' Euan shrugged as the words he had never intended to share fell like stones into the air between them. 'My mother took her own life. The year after Fi died.'

'Oh…my God…'

The look he was getting now was more than one of pity. It was the look of someone who was shocked and hurting on his behalf. Someone who cared about what had happened to him and who he was. Someone who cared far too much.

'Oh, Euan… I'm so, so sorry…'

He couldn't let Abby continue to look at him like this, with tears beginning to make her eyes shimmer. She couldn't be allowed to care about him like this. Because he couldn't accept it. He didn't want those kinds of feelings in his life. And he knew he could control them. God knew he'd worked hard enough for too many years not to have learned how to do that. Already, they were back through that door and all he needed to do was make sure it was firmly shut. It wasn't Abby that was going to walk out on this conversation. To walk away from whatever closeness they had generated between them in the last few days.

It was Euan.

And that was exactly what he did.

CHAPTER TEN

ABBY COULD FEEL the distance growing between them with every step that Euan took as he left the library, and that distance wasn't simply physical. He was pulling down the shutters. Making sure that any chink she had found in his emotional barriers was being rapidly repaired.

The worst thing was, she couldn't blame him. Not at all.

Discovering the reason that nobody talked about Euan's mother had been so shocking she'd had no idea what to say. Or do. And then, as she watched him leave, Abby realised that she had already said and done far too much. It might have been totally unintentional but she had reopened old wounds for both Euan and his grandmother. Deeper wounds than the ones she had known about that had been caused by the tragic deaths of both Euan's father and his beloved little sister. A dark wound that must, at some level, have felt like an abandonment to a grieving teenager.

For a long, long minute and then another, Abby simply stood there alone in the library, as a pain like nothing she was familiar with grew in her heart until it felt heavy enough to be pulling her down. She had hurt Euan and Maggie but she was also feeling a pain that felt very personal because, although it had been such an astonishingly short space of time, instinct was telling her very firmly that she had found her own family in Ravenswood Castle.

She had met two children who had completely captured her heart. A tradition of celebrating Christmas in a way she could have happily embraced herself for as many years as she had ahead of her. A man that she just knew she could have loved for the rest of her life. And an amazing grandmother who was everything Abby had always aspired to be. A strong, brave woman who was so generous, so compassionate that she had endless love to share. Abby finally stirred herself to go to where she knew Margaret McKendry was likely to be. She was in need of a smidgeon of that love for herself right now.

Maggie was in the kitchen, as expected, sitting at the enormous, old, scrubbed pine table with a cup of tea in front of her and a small girl, with curly red hair, half asleep on her knee. Liam was sitting at the table as well, a plate with a half-eaten gingerbread man on it in front of him. Abby could see instantly that there was something different about him but it took a heartbeat to realise what it was.

He wasn't scowling. Or avoiding eye contact. He was, in fact, looking directly at Abby as she came into the kitchen. A steady look that was all too easy to read. He might not believe it was actually going to happen but he was trusting Abby to keep the promise she'd made. She knew how big a deal this was. If she broke that trust, it would most likely never be offered again. To anyone.

An already heavy heart had just got even heavier. When Lucy held her arms up to offer Abby a cuddle, it was too much of a mission to blink away the tears in time as she stooped to press her face against those soft curls for a kiss. And, of course, Maggie noticed.

'That grandson of mine.' She made a 'tutting' sound of sympathy as her gaze met Abby's. 'He's gone off by himself again, hasn't he?'

'Mmm.' Abby couldn't trust herself to say anything more. She sank into the chair beside Maggie. Even being this close to the older woman was making her feel a little better—as if strength came as a bonus with that understanding and love.

Maggie didn't say anything more, either. Instead, she cuddled Lucy. 'Do you know what the other children are doing at the moment?'

'No.'

'They're making stockings. Do you know what stockings are?'

Lucy shook her head.

'I do,' Liam said. 'They're really big socks.'

'They are,' Maggie agreed. 'Special red socks, these ones. You know our Cath who cooks all our food? Well, her mother has some friends who have a knitting circle and they work hard to knit these stockings and collect things that they help the children sew onto them to make them pretty. And then they embroider your name on them and you can keep them for ever. That's what's happening in the drawing room at the moment.'

'Aren't you supposed to hang them somewhere like on a door handle?' Liam asked.

'Absolutely.' Abby nodded.

'We hang them on the fireplace in the drawing room,' Maggie told him. 'It's big enough for everybody's stockings.'

'Do they have presents inside them on Christmas morning?'

'They most certainly do.' Maggie nodded.

Lucy's eyes were very wide. 'What sort of presents?'

Again, that steady gaze of Liam's was on Abby. 'Maybe the sort of presents that you ask Father Christmas for when you write a letter,' he suggested.

Maggie blinked, catching Abby's gaze as they both acknowledged the plea behind his words.

Lucy was sliding off Maggie's lap. 'I want to make a stocking,' she said. 'Please?'

Maggie smiled at Liam. 'Do you think you could take Lucy into the drawing room? The knitting ladies will be very happy to help you both make a stocking if you want. Dr Abby and I have a few very important phone calls that we need to make.'

Liam suddenly looked a lot older than his ten years as he nodded slowly. It felt as though he understood that those phone calls would be how Abby was going to be able to answer his plea and keep the promise she'd made. As if he knew, all too well, that his and Lucy's futures could well rest on the outcome of discussions with authorities.

'Come on, Luce.' He held out his hand. 'I'll look after you.'

As soon as the children had left the library, Maggie put her telephone on speaker mode and made their first call.

'Judith? It's Maggie McKendry here. I hope your father is still improving?'

'He is. Thank you. I'm so glad you called, Maggie. I've been worried about calling you with that bad news about Liam and Lucy earlier. I just wish I could do something.'

'You know what?' Maggie smiled at Abby as she spoke. 'Christmas is all about making wishes come true, isn't it? I think we might be able to work together to make one happen to change that bad news into something rather miraculous.'

The tears that Maggie was brushing away as they fell were melting Abby's heart and it took only another shared glance for the bond that was forming between them to feel strong enough to be invincible. They both loved Liam and Lucy and would do whatever they could to keep them together.

And they both loved Euan McKendry. Abby couldn't tell Maggie that she now knew the dreadful secret about his mother because she'd caused enough grief already in reopening old wounds. But Maggie knew he'd taken himself off again and she was clearly aware that he would be using his time alone to repair his emotional barricades. They might have both been shut out of trying to help him get through something that was overwhelming but they could support each other. And Euan, when or if he got to a point when he would allow them to get closer.

'I'm aware that we're running out of time today,' Maggie continued, 'but you'll know exactly who we need to talk to and it would be such a gift to all of us if we could at least get an agreement in principle today. Do you remember Abby who was here when you brought the children to the castle?'

'Of course. She's lovely. I could see that Lucy warmed to her straight away.'

'It was mutual,' Maggie said. 'And it's grown to a very special bond. I've got Abby here with me now, Judith, and what we want to try and make happen is to not let that bond get broken. Between Lucy and Abby but even more between Lucy and Liam. And I'm behind it a thousand per cent. I can be sure that the whole village of Kirkwood will be behind it.'

'Oh, my…' They could hear Judith's intake of breath. 'I think I can guess what you're going to say but tell me everything and I'll do whatever I can to help.'

The Christmas stockings had been finished, with a child's name embroidered on white trim at the top and the rest decorated with knitted snowflakes and Christmas trees, stars and baubles along with tiny golden bells. They'd been hung from the mantelpiece over the huge, open fire in the drawing room and were quite the distraction for a final carol singing practice before everyone got ready to be ferried down to the village church in a convoy of volunteer's cars.

Lucy's angel dress was looking distinctly grubby after the game of hide and seek in the old rowboat, and the wings were even more droopy, but she was still determined to wear them.

'You'll need warm tights on under that dress, sweetheart,' Abby told her. 'And you'll have to have your pink coat on top. There's more snow out there tonight and it's very, very cold.'

'Can I still wear my wings?'

'Of course you can.' Abby had to give her another cuddle and she met Maggie's eyes over the top of those soft, red curls. 'It's the best night of all to be wearing angel wings.'

They were still waiting to hear back from the person who had the power to make their own Christmas wish come true but everyone, starting with Judith and then stepping up through the Social Services administration levels, had been cautiously optimistic.

We'll get back to you as soon as we can, they'd said. *But with it being Christmas Day tomorrow you'll understand that we can't make any promises about how quickly that will be.'*

'You go and get yourself ready,' Maggie told Abby. 'I'll finish getting this poppet into her coat and wings and hat.'

Abby nodded. 'I won't be long.' She paused beside the door. 'Have you seen…? She paused and then bit her lip as Maggie shook her head.

Abby went into her room and began to change her clothes. She'd brought two dresses with her to the castle—a red one that would be perfect for Christmas Day and another that wasn't seasonal but it was one of her favourite dresses ever and it was lovely and warm, being a dark blue, wool knit with folds of soft fabric that reached the top of her long boots. It even had a hood so she wouldn't need to add a hat. She had warm tights to wear under it, as well, just like those Lucy would be wearing under her angel dress. Abby brushed her hair but left it loose and then hurried to find her coat so that she was ready to join the excited children and carers who were gathering in the foyer.

She put on a bright smile as she went downstairs but she was sadly getting used to her heart feeling too heavy. Abby had been looking forward so much to the carol service in the old, stone village church this evening, with Euan playing the bagpipes to lead the children in and Maggie had been sure that he'd turn up in time.

'He's never missed a single Christmas Eve,' she'd told Abby between two of the many phone calls they'd made that afternoon. *'Not since the very first time when it was just our Fi and wee Jamie who wanted to sing a carol.'*

'What did they sing?'

'"We Wish You a Merry Christmas".'

The wry smile they'd shared had said it all. That this Christmas was in danger of not being as merry as any of them might have wished.

But Maggie was there, now, at the bottom of the stairs, in the midst of a group of people that she'd brought together to have the merriest Christmas that she could create and she had a bright smile on her face, too. Abby was suddenly quite confident that she could give her best this evening, no matter what. Because Maggie was here. Because this remarkable woman had found a way to create joy despite the many challenges that life had thrown at her.

And because Abby believed the words she'd thrown at Euan this afternoon—that the only way to find the joy was to risk the heartbreak of loving. And there was so much love, right here, with Liam standing beside Maggie, holding his little sister's hand.

'Come with us,' Maggie said. 'Fergus has brought his car to take us to church.'

They gathered again at the rectory right beside the old church where the pastor's wife would tell them when the village congregation was gathered and ready for the children to be led in. In the absence of the traditional piping in, Muriel was going to fill the gap and play 'The Little Drummer Boy' on the organ.

The candles didn't have real flames, but the glow of the small lights was enough to be charming in the darkness of a snowy, Scottish evening. They lined up near the arched doorway. Callum, in his wheelchair, was supposed to be first but Milo was too excited to stay behind him and nobody minded. The pastor's wife peeped into the church where silence had fallen and she was about to beckon them in, when the silence was broken.

Not by any of the waiting children. It was a sound that came from around the corner of the church. A sound they all recognised because they'd heard it before, in the drawing room of Ravenswood Castle, no less. The squeak and drone of a set of bagpipes being primed to respond to the piper. The setting of the base notes that the tune of the song would dance on top of.

As the first notes of the song became clear, the piper stepped around the corner of Kirkwood's church and came towards them, the pipes under his arm and a soft drift of snow-flakes overhead.

Abby had known that it would be Euan McKendry—from that first deep sound that sent a thrill right into her bones. A sound that encompassed the rich history of this northern country along with the mystery of a proud man who kept too much, too close to his heart and intended to keep facing life alone.

Yes, Abby had expected to see the man she was so in love with. What she hadn't expected to see was that he would be wearing formal, Scottish attire. A kilt with a background that was dark green and a long swathe of the same tartan draped over one shoulder and fastened with a big, silver brooch. Long white socks and black shoes and even a leather sporran that hung from his hips with a chain.

Even more unexpected was the way Abby's heart felt as if it had stopped. That the whole world stopped turning for that missed heartbeat, as she realised that, no matter how much love she had around her, her life would always have an enormous Euan-shaped gap in it if he wasn't close to her.

She'd never experienced a feeling of being in love like this. Surely something powerful enough to make her wonder if the world really had stopped spinning for that moment couldn't be purely one-sided?

Following Milo's example, most of the children were putting their fingers in their ears as Euan walked slowly past and into the church. Lucy buried her face against Liam, who put his own hands over her ears. Abby didn't cover hers. If anything, she stood a little straighter and waited for the moment she knew would come—when Euan would meet her steady gaze. He was about three footfalls away when he did and he held her gaze until his next step put her behind him. Abby could see that he was at one with the music he was playing, using it as a shield from the outside world. But she could also see that he *saw* her.

And that she wasn't wrong in believing that she wasn't the only one captured by a love like no other. Maybe Euan wasn't ready or willing to admit it but that certainty that it was there was enough for Abby for the moment. Enough to bring a smile to her lips and a shine to her eyes as she sat with the children in the prettiest, stone church and sang the Christmas carols she'd known and loved all her life.

It was enough to keep her smiling as she

got caught up in the happy chaos of getting all the children back to the castle and given supper and then the excitement of putting some hay out for the reindeer, mince pies for Santa and a last, lingering look at the magic of all the fairy lights adorning the grand, old castle. It took a while to settle the children into bed, of course, but they all knew the sooner they were asleep, the sooner the joy of Christmas Day would begin.

After the children were tucked up and sleeping, the adults had more work to do. The special gifts from families were placed under the Christmas tree in the drawing room. Stockings were filled with small treats and toys and a sack was stuffed with the extra things that Fergus, in his Santa suit, would distribute after Christmas dinner. Parents and carers took a couple of small things, like books and games, to put under the little trees in everyone's rooms. With a bit of luck, they told each other, it might mean they could catch a few minutes of extra sleep in the morning.

It was getting close to midnight when Abby wrapped her last parcel and put it into Santa's sack for Lucy—a fluffy toy donkey she'd managed to secretly buy, along with the dog for Leah, because it would remind Lucy of the donkeys she loved at Ravenswood Castle. And how easy had that been? A shared glance with a secret message—the kind parents no doubt became experts in—and Euan had distracted both the children by taking them to watch an animated display of Santa's elves in his workshop on the other side of the toy shop. Good grief…had it only been early this afternoon? So much had happened today.

So much had changed.

She hadn't expected to see Euan helping with any of these Christmas Eve activities but it was surprising that she hadn't seen him anywhere in the castle since they'd come back from the church. Come to think of it, she hadn't noticed him at all in the bustle of getting children into cars before they could get too cold or the road could become too covered in snow. She'd been in doctor mode at that time, as well, watching every child carefully and speaking to the carers to make sure they were coping with the stress that excitement could bring.

Maggie had needed watching as well. She was very clearly tired and in pain by late in the evening after the children had been settled and Abby made sure she had taken her painkillers and then sent her to bed as soon as they were having an obvious effect.

'You need to get as much rest as possible,' Abby had told her firmly, a couple of hours ago. 'It's the day we've all been waiting for tomorrow and…it's *your* day.' She wrapped her arms around Maggie. 'The day you've created every year for so many years, to bring happiness to so many people. You're amazing, do you know that?' She kissed Maggie's soft cheek. 'I love you so much.'

'Oh…lovie… I wish it was true. I wish I *could* bring happiness to everyone. Or at least happiness that will last longer than just one day. Especially to you, right now, because if anyone deserves to be truly happy, it's someone with a heart like yours.'

Euan also deserved that kind of happiness, Abby thought, as she finally headed towards her own room in the closing minutes of Christmas Eve. And they'd found it, hadn't they? At least for a while. This last couple of nights together had taken them somewhere that was as far away from any sadness and memories of suffering and loss as anyone could get. They had found a place that only they could be. A language no one else in the world could speak and the joy in that communication had been astonishing.

Would he let her get that close again? The look he'd given her, as he'd walked past her at the church, had sent a silent message that strongly suggested he wanted to let her come that close. But was he still angry with her? Enough to deny them even one last night together?

She went past the door to her own room and on to the end of the hallway to the side of the house where she knew one of the towers of this magical castle would be shaping the walls of Euan's bedroom. She tapped lightly on the door and then again, but she didn't want to disturb anyone else, especially Maggie, who wasn't that far away, so, instead of knocking more loudly, she turned the handle of the door and opened it carefully.

There was a lamp glowing on the bedside table. She could see the round wall with a beautifully arched window with a stone sill that was deep enough to function as a window seat. She could see a four-poster bed like the one in her room, and a rich, Persian style carpet over the wooden floorboards. A fireplace was set but not lit. A door stood open to reveal an unoccupied bathroom. The covers of the bed had been turned down but it was empty.

The whole room was empty.

Any confidence Abby had of what she'd read in that gaze as Euan had walked past her playing his bagpipes evaporated and her chest tightened so painfully, it was impossible to take in a new breath.

It was Christmas Day.

And Euan hadn't come home.

CHAPTER ELEVEN

STONE WAS NOT the best material for a window seat in Scotland on a snowy winter's night. Abby had no idea how long she'd sat there, watching the swirl of flakes outside as she waited...*hoping*...that Euan would return. The cold was seeping further and further into her body and it felt as if it were finally reaching vital, internal organs.

Like her heart.

She could go and warm up by climbing into her own bed but what was the point when she knew there was no hope of getting any sleep? She would be too acutely aware that Euan wasn't sharing her bed, and lying there alone in the dark, missing him so much, would make it even harder to stop her thoughts going in directions she was determined not to let them go.

It would be so easy to sink into misery

and start believing that this was going to be her worst Christmas ever. That the pain of heartbreak that was hovering like the darkest of clouds could spoil everything, but how stupid would that be? She'd come to Ravenswood Castle absolutely convinced that this was going to be her best Christmas ever—because she was going to spend it with children and that was what Christmas was all about. Children who needed the kind of care she was able to provide. The unexpected bonus of spending these special days in a castle that looked as if it were a fairy tale come to life was magical, and to be experiencing her very first white Christmas was the icing on an extraordinary cake.

None of those things had changed. If anything, they'd just got better. Way more significant. She'd found Maggie. And Liam and Lucy. And a place that felt achingly like the home she'd been searching for without realising it. She was taking steps to an unexpected but meaningful future that she hoped, with all her heart, would make this place, and these people, a part of her life for ever.

Was she going to let the fact that Euan didn't want—or, more likely, simply wasn't able—to be a part of this new future tarnish the joy of everything else?

No, she absolutely wasn't.

The stiffness from the chill in Abby's limbs began to wear off as she walked past her room, down the stairs, towards the kitchen where she had every intention of making herself a very large mug of hot chocolate. She'd also go hunting for some of Cath's delicious shortbread, she decided, because just thinking about it was enough to imagine the taste. As she reached the kitchen, however, and saw the thick flurry of snowflakes reflected in the light shining out through the windows, Abby remembered standing on that street in Inverness and being so tempted to open her mouth and stick out her tongue to try and catch some of those flakes to see what they tasted like.

It was enough to make her smile. To recapture some of the joy she'd feared she was losing and…what the heck? There was nobody around to see her behaving like a child so Abby let herself out of the back door into the kitchen garden, wrapping her arms around her body to stave off the cold. She tipped her head back and stuck out her tongue and found it was easy enough to catch snowflakes. They might be nothing more than semi-frozen water but they tasted exactly how she'd imagined they would. They were flavoured with magic...

Not that she could stand out here too long. It was time to put the kettle on and make a hot drink. But as Abby turned to go back inside she heard a very odd noise. Not unlike one of Euan's grunts when he didn't want to say anything but it was a lot louder and longer. Abby looked around the garden, softly lit by the lights she'd turned on in the kitchen, half expecting to see a fox, perhaps. Or a deer? The sound came again as she looked and she realised it was coming from the section of the old stables that was still being used for animals rather than the clinic. Where the horses and donkeys and other farmyard pets were kept in their warm stalls at night. Abby knew she had to go and check what was happening. She hadn't grown up on a farm without developing an instinct that was telling her quite clearly that something wasn't right, here.

There was a musty warmth behind the thick stone walls of the stables, with the smell of the animals mixed with the deep layers of fresh straw in all the stalls and pens. Abby turned on lights that only provided a few pools of illumination but, while some of the inhabitants stirred sleepily at the interruption, there was one stall that was clearly the source of the unusual sounds. Mary the donkey was rolling on her back when Abby opened the top half of the door. Then she got to her feet and paced around the space, stopping to arch her back and make another grunting noise.

'Oh…' Abby caught her bottom lip between her teeth. 'You're in labour, aren't you?'

She glanced at her watch. It was nearly one a.m. She couldn't go and wake Maggie when she'd been in too much stress when she wasn't well and was in so much need of as much rest as she could get. There was no point in waking anybody else, nor was there any need to call a vet unless there was a problem with the birth and there were no signs to suggest that might be the case at this point in time. Abby's experience of helping lambs and calves into the world, on the farm alongside her father, was more than enough to ensure she could recognise when or if things were not shaping up to go well.

On the other hand, she couldn't leave Mary to give birth alone, in case problems did develop, so Abby turned on a wall heater above the cleaning area with the sinks and buckets full of brushes and rags and cupboards full of stable necessities and positioned herself on the pile of nearby straw bales that allowed her to see into Mary's stall. There was a pile of old horse blankets in a wheelbarrow in this corner of the stables as well, so she took a couple of those, one to cover the loosely tied bales and give her a soft surface to sit on and the other to wrap around her shoulders to keep warm, because it was going to take a long time for that heater to make any real difference to the temperature inside these stone walls.

Abby had no idea how long a donkey's labour might take. Mary was restless, lying down often, only to get up and start pacing again. Joseph, who was in the neighbouring stall, seemed uninterested in what was happening, even when the first signs of the birth were obvious and the white membranes of the sac enclosing the foal could be seen under Mary's tail.

'I'm here,' Abby told Mary. 'I won't leave you alone. You're doing well.'

Knowing that a new life was going to appear very soon gave Abby another flash of that joy she'd thought was tarnished and she hugged that to her heart as she watched over the donkey. Mary was lying down again and the contractions were coming close together. Abby could see part of the front legs and hooves of the baby through the mist of the membranes. She pulled the blanket closer around herself, remembering icy spring mornings on the high-country New Zealand farm she'd grown up on, as she helped her father deliver lambs.

She'd never wanted to be a farmer herself, maybe because of that loneliness she'd been so aware of as an only child, so it was ironic, she realised, that here she was in the highlands of a country on the opposite side of the world, with a dwelling that was so huge it had whole wings closed up because there were too many rooms, and yet Abby had never felt less lonely in her whole life. There was so much love here she could feel it even being by herself out here in the stables in the middle of the night. Love that had everything to do with Maggie, who was the most extraordinary woman she'd ever met, and with Lucy and Liam, of course. And, even if it was never going to come to anything more, a huge part of that love—maybe most of it—had everything to do with Euan, from the courageous, loving boy he'd been to the proud but scarred man he was today.

Her breath caught in her throat at that point as she realised something that seemed suddenly so very clear. So simple. If only Euan could realise that it was letting that love, that was here in such abundance, *in* that could heal his heart, not shutting it out as he'd spent so much of his life trying to do to protect himself. She had to blink away tears then, and as she did so she could see that Mary was getting tired. Her legs were sticking out straight and she was arching her back with each contraction but her breathing was getting laboured and, when she tried to lift her head, she simply let it drop onto the straw again. The foal's face was visible now, with its nose resting on the front legs.

Abby climbed down from the straw pile. Mary needed help. Maybe more help than Abby could provide alone but she didn't have to wonder where she might find that extra help from because, in almost the same instant as the thought was forming, she felt the brush of freshly cold air as someone opened one of the outer stable doors.

No…it wasn't just 'someone'.

It was the one person that Abby had been desperately hoping to see when she'd been sitting alone in his room, hours ago now.

'Euan...' Abby couldn't help herself. She had to go to him. As if she was perfectly confident he would want nothing more than to take her into his arms. She even held out her own arms so that she would be ready to wrap them around his neck as soon as she was close enough.

And...maybe this was her first Christmas miracle, because taking her into his arms was exactly what Euan did.

Oh...the shape of her as he took her into his arms...

As though it was filling every empty corner in his life.

That warmth. The scent of her hair. That feeling of the joy of simply being alive and not being alone.

Euan held Abby close against his own body. And she wrapped her arms around his neck in a gesture that was pure Abby—ready to give so much love. And maybe forgiveness, as well? He'd pushed her away and that must have felt like a totally undeserved rejection.

He pressed his cheek against her hair. 'I'm so sorry,' he said. 'I needed…some time…to get my head around all of this…'

To grapple with a flood of emotion that had been threatening to drown him for days now. Ever since he'd come home to what could have meant facing up to losing Maggie. To the usual battle his childhood home represented, of pushing ghosts back into the past where they belonged and the extra, unexpected challenge of coping with what seemed like a reflection of his own early life in Liam and Lucy. And, on top of that, to the irresistible pull towards a woman he'd believed was completely wrong for him and who could never be allowed to be a part of his life.

How wrong could someone be?

Abby was exactly what he desperately needed in his life if he was to keep feeling this…*whole*…

'I know.' Abby pulled back just far enough that he could see the depth of understanding in her eyes. And…miraculously, the love that was still there. 'It's okay…you're here now and…it's perfect timing. I *need* you, Euan.'

He tightened the band of his arms around her. 'I'm here.' He pressed a kiss against her hair this time and was about to tell her how much he needed *her* and how he would always be here but Abby pulled away.

'No… I *really* need you. For Mary.'

'Mary?' For a split-second Euan had no idea what Abby was talking about and then it clicked. They were in the stables. 'The *donkey*?'

'She's in labour. I think she's in trouble.'

Maybe Abby only needed him so urgently because of Mary but, for now, that was enough. She needed him and he wouldn't want to be anywhere else. He opened the lower door of the stall and they both went to the exhausted donkey lying in the straw.

'You hold her head and talk to her,' Euan said. 'I'll pull with the next contractions. The sooner this baby is born, the better.'

If it was even still alive. Euan could see the foal's head inside the broken membrane and there was no sign of life. He put some straw in his hands to help get a grip on the forelegs that had punctured the sac and, as Mary's legs stiffened again, he pulled, gently increasing the pressure as the contraction continued. Abby was lying in the straw with her arms around Mary's neck, applying some counter pressure and talking reassuringly to the jenny at the same time.

'It's okay, Mary. You're doing really, really well. Euan's here now and your baby's going to be okay too. Just one more big push…'

It took several more pushes and, when the baby finally slipped out, there were still no signs of life. Mary tried to lift her head to look at the foal but she fell back and lay there panting, almost as limp as her newborn.

Abby was on her knees, still stroking Mary's head but her gaze was fixed on the foal. Then she looked up to meet Euan's gaze and he could see the distress in her eyes. He could feel it himself. She thought it was hopeless, didn't she? Euan didn't say anything aloud, he just held her gaze a heartbeat longer, so that she could know what he was thinking.

I can't promise a happy ever after but I can promise I'll do the absolute best I can… Every time…

He pulled away the shreds of membrane covering the foal's face to make sure the nose and mouth were clear and then he grabbed big handfuls of clean straw to rub its body and stimulate circulation. He could feel Abby watching. He could almost feel that she was holding her breath. Holding that huge heart of hers in her hands.

And then it happened. The foal twitched. The small chest expanded as it took its first breath and then its eyes opened. Mary could feel the movement behind her and, this time, she managed to raise her head for long enough to see her baby.

'I'll bring the foal close enough for her to lick,' Euan said, gathering the long-legged baby into his arms. 'It's a girl,' he told Abby. 'And isn't she gorgeous?'

'She's adorable.' Abby's smile was joyous. 'I'm so happy she's okay. That you arrived just in time. I couldn't have done that on my own.'

Again, Euan wanted to tell her that he could always be here and that she would never need to be alone again, but so many years of practice in deflecting emotions made him retreat to safer, practical, things to say. 'We'll need to watch them both for a while, to make sure they've bonded and the placenta's arrived. Bring one of those blankets and we'll cover Mary until she's rested enough.'

'There's a good place for us to sit and watch,' Abby told him. 'Where I've been for most of the night, up on the straw pile.

Close enough to help but far enough not to be interfering.'

A few minutes later, that was where they both were. Snuggled into a nest of straw. Euan pulled a blanket around their shoulders.

'It's not exactly clean but I think we've ruined our clothes anyway.'

'I don't care.' Abby's face was shining with joy again. 'Look…'

Euan had to make himself look away from her face as he felt a new rush of emotion that had nothing to do with the donkeys. Mary had rolled onto her stomach, with her legs tucked beneath her, and she was licking her foal from head to foot, including the pair of ears that this baby would need a lot of time to grow into.

'I think they've bonded,' Abby whispered.

Euan shifted his gaze back to her face and he was smiling as he leaned in to kiss her. Slowly. Gently. The donkey mother and child weren't the only creatures to be sealing their bond here.

'Merry Christmas,' he whispered. 'I'm sorry I haven't got a gift for you.'

Abby's lips wobbled as she tried to smile back. 'Being with you is the only gift I need,' she said. 'I thought… I thought I'd lost you.'

'I nearly lost myself,' Euan confessed. 'I've been sitting in my car for hours and it felt like I was in a fight for my life.'

'And you were alone...' Abby touched his face. Such a gentle touch but it still conveyed exactly how much she cared.

'I think I had to be. There was so much that I'd shut away for so long because I didn't want to feel the pain that came with them and it needed to come out. So many things I needed to remember. And feel...'

'Like what?'

'Like my mother and her floaty dresses and all her bangles and how soft her hands were. I'll tell you all about her one day.' Euan swallowed hard. 'And I remembered how I'd watch Fiona in her bassinette. She wasn't expected to live at all but she was a wee fighter and I'd sit there and wait for her to open her eyes and I'd tell her to keep fighting. That I'd look after her. I'd watch her go blue and struggle to breathe but, every time, she'd get through and they gave her the first operation when she was three weeks old.' Euan was finding it a bit of a struggle to take a new breath himself. 'So, there I was fielding the punches and kicks that came with every memory and wondering how much pain it would take before it killed me. It took until I felt as exhausted as poor Mary down there but then...'

'What?' Abby had snuggled down to tuck her head in the hollow beneath his collarbone as he was speaking and her voice was a whisper against his neck. A warm puff of her breath and the tickle of her lips against his skin. 'Tell me...'

'I thought of you. No, that's not quite true. You were there all along—in my head. In my heart. But I'd been pushing you away. Ever since you'd told me that if I couldn't let love into my life I wasn't really living. That I'd never feel the joy. And then you'd asked me about my mother...'

'I'm so sorry.' There were tears in Abby's eyes. 'I had no idea...'

'Of course you didn't. We never talk about it. Because that's when I shut myself off from living. And that's what I was thinking about. That you were right. That I *was* actually scared of feeling that joy and... I might never have felt it again if it wasn't for you coming here. You give that joy so freely, Abby—that love. And you do it without hesitation even though it could mean that your heart will get broken again and again. You're prepared to do that for Lucy *and* for Liam, when you know how hard it might be, and that kind of courage is one of the things I love so much about you.'

One of the things…?

Love…?

Had Euan just told her that he loved her?

Abby had to tune in again to the soft words that were continuing.

'…and aye, it might have been painful, but I think you've brought me back to life, Abby Hawkins…' Euan's smile was wry as he looked down. 'I think I knew I was in trouble the moment I found you on the castle doorstep.'

'Oh…' Abby lifted her head so that she could meet Euan's gaze but she lost her words as she saw the way he was looking back at her. She could drown in the love she could see in the misty grey of his eyes. She needed to find more of the oxygen that seemed to be in short supply around here, and when she opened her mouth to take a gulp of air the words were there, after all.

'I love you,' she whispered. 'I love you so much, Euan McKendry.'

And this had to be her second Christmas

miracle—that Euan had found a way forward. That, given time and care, his heart could really be healed.

And yes, maybe they still wanted very different things in their futures but, right now, that didn't seem to matter, because this was like the time they'd found together when they'd shut the bedroom door behind them. The place where they could just be. Where they could find the joy that was bright enough to banish any shadows.

'I love you,' Euan murmured, 'even more...'

One kiss led to another. Slow, gentle kisses and long, shared glances that held the promise of everything, including enough time to let it all fall into place. And then they simply held each other, tucked into the warmth of that nest of straw, until they drifted into sleep, their bodies so close it was impossible to tell whether it was their own heartbeat or each other's that they could feel. And it didn't matter, anyway, because being that close was all that either of them wanted for now.

'Oh...look... Can you see?' Maggie couldn't lift Lucy high enough to see over the stable door without it being too painful, so she opened it instead.

'It's a baby...' Lucy was awestruck. 'A baby *donkey*. A Christmas baby donkey...'

Liam had a tight hold of his sister's hand. 'Don't get too close, Luce. The mum won't like that.'

'Mothers do protect their babies,' Maggie agreed. 'Mary's very gentle but we won't ask to pat the baby just yet. It must have been born in the middle of the night, I think. She's all dry and fluffy already and look...she's having a drink of milk.'

But Liam wasn't looking at the foal. He was staring at the straw pile where something was moving under a blanket.

'Oh...' Again, Maggie's exclamation was heartfelt. 'So that's where you are. I came looking for you both, when Liam and Lucy wanted to open their stockings.'

She'd never seen her grandson looking so dishevelled. And Abby had straw in her hair and was blinking sleep from her eyes but she'd never looked so beautiful. Seeing the two of them, together, filled Maggie's heart with hope. If only they knew how much they needed each other.

'And I needed to find you, too. I got a message, late last night, after I was asleep so I only saw it this morning. A message from Judith.'

She could hear Abby's sharp inward breath as she realised how significant the next words she would hear would be. She saw the way her gaze flew to meet Euan's, as if she was looking for strength, and Maggie's heart gave a huge squeeze as she saw the way he was meeting that gaze and the way his fingers were curling around Abby's as he took hold of her hand. It was so obvious that he was letting her know that he was there for her. That what she was hoping for was just as important to him.

That he loved her...

'It's been approved,' she said quietly. 'There's interviews and paperwork to be sorted, of course, but, in principle, everybody's on board.' She took a deep breath, looking down at Lucy and then across to Liam before looking back to Abby. 'I thought you'd like to tell them yourself.'

It was Liam that Abby focused on. 'You know what this means, don't you?'

Liam shrugged. 'Maybe...'

'It means that we're both going to take care of Lucy. Together. And, if I can, I'm going to adopt you both.' She held out an arm towards

Lucy. 'Is that okay, sweetheart? Can I look after you and love you and be your mum?'

Lucy didn't have to speak. Her answer was obvious by the way she let go of Maggie's hand to start scrambling up the pile of straw and into Abby's lap for a cuddle.

'So…we're going to stay here?' Liam sounded dubious. 'At the castle?'

'If that's still okay with Maggie. Otherwise we'll find a wee house of our own.'

'Don't be daft,' Maggie said. 'Of course you're going to stay here. I want to be part of this family.'

'Me, too.'

Maggie's breath caught. She could feel the tension in the way Liam was holding himself as well. Even Abby and Lucy had gone very still. They all turned to focus on the person who'd just spoken with such sincerity.

Euan…

It was Lucy who broke the stunned silence.

'Are you going to be my daddy, then?'

It was Liam who answered. 'That would only work if they got married. Him and Dr Abby.'

'That's true.' Euan nodded.

'And you can't get married.' Liam shook his head. 'Not unless you really love someone.'

'That's also true,' Euan agreed. 'But you know what?'

'What?'

Maggie was holding her breath as Liam asked the question she also wanted the answer to.

'I do. I really, really love Dr Abby.'

'Me too.' Lucy wound her arms around Abby's neck to cuddle her, but Abby was looking past that cloud of red curls to hold Euan's gaze.

'And I really, really love Dr Euan,' she said.

'So…' Liam was almost scowling as he stared at them both. 'You're going to get married, then? And we're going to be your kids? For ever? Even if you have kids of your own?'

Euan held Abby's gaze for a heartbeat longer before he shifted it to let it settle on Liam. Long enough for Maggie to see that there were no barriers between Abby and Euan now. That the possibilities for their shared future seemed without limits. They might well have their own bairns. They might even carry on with Ravenswood Castle's Christmas camp for sick children, but they were going to trust each other and take it one step at a time.

Euan's smile for Liam gave the impression of offering a pact. 'How 'bout we get used to being a family first and then we'll talk about getting married? But I promise you, we're not going anywhere. This is home now, okay?'

Liam nodded slowly. He was watching Euan begin to climb down from the straw. Maggie could sense that Liam was close to tears as the news that he and Lucy were not going to be separated began to sink in. She put her arm around his shoulders and drew him close to her side.

'It's about time we went inside, don't you think? I do believe there are some Christmas stockings to open.' Euan touched Liam's shoulder as he drew close enough and lowered his voice. This was a man-to-man communication but Maggie could still hear it. 'Lucy might need her big brother's help to climb down. That straw can be a bit slippery.'

Maggie could feel the way Liam's shoulders straightened and her heart filled with pride as he went to look after his little sister. She already loved this lad with all her heart. The thought that she could well have many years ahead of her, after she got that pesky surgery out of the way, to win Liam's trust and hopefully his love filled her with as much joy as the knowledge that Abby and Euan had, without doubt, found the person they were meant to be with. Their life partner. A soul mate.

You only had to catch a glimpse of the way they were looking at each other to know that they were both the happiest people on earth right now. But so was Maggie, come to that. This was the first time she'd ever seen Liam smiling as well and Lucy... Maggie was feeling even more misty. Abby had probably lit up whole rooms with her happiness just like Lucy when she was a little girl because she was still doing it now. The love that was filling this ancient building in this moment was, in fact, well...it was nothing short of a Christmas miracle, that was what it was.

'I had a feeling that this was going to happen.' Everybody was looking at Maggie as she wiped away a few happy tears. She turned to lead them all back to the warmth of the castle. Into their home. Everybody would be up by now and the celebrations would be well under way. She could imagine the excited faces of children who still believed in the magic. She still believed in that magic herself—who wouldn't after what had already happened so early on this special day? A glance over her shoulder showed Lucy holding Liam's hand on one side and Abby's on the other. Abby's free hand was being held by Euan.

They looked like a family.

They *were* a family now. And Maggie was blessed to be a part of it.

She was just thinking aloud but her words were loud enough for everyone to hear.

'This is going to be the best Christmas *ever.*'

* * * * *